ALSO BY MARIAN THURM

Floating (Stories)
Walking Distance
These Things Happen (Stories)
Henry in Love
The Way We Live Now
The Clairvoyant
What's Come Over You? (Stories)

UNDER THE NAME LUCY JACKSON

Posh
Slicker

TODAY IS NOT YOUR DAY

STORIES

MARIAN THURM

(sixoneseven)BOOKS

Permissions requests may be addressed to
SixOneSeven Books
21 Wormwood Street
Ste. 325
Boston, MA 02210
www.sixonesevenbooks.com

Cover design by Whitney Scharer.

New York / Marian Thurm — First Edition
ISBN 978-0-9831505-5-8

Printed in the United States of America

In loving memory of my dear friends
Barbi Kantor–Goldenberg
and Shirley Zucker

CONTENTS

WHAT WENT ON

NOT TO PAT MYSELF ON THE BACK or anything, but the fact is that when my ex-husband's hot young wife fell ill recently, I went over there the day Miranda was released from the hospital and cooked them an excellent dinner. On their high-tech stainless steel stove, I sautéed chicken cutlets in butter and shallots and prepared a big fragrant pot of basmati rice. I even brought over a bottle of white wine, poured a glass for each of them, lit a pair of long, tapered candles and positioned them just so at the center of the dining-room table, the very table, as it happens, which formerly stood on an oriental rug in my dining room. Months before the divorce officially came through and Rick and I were in the process of dividing up our things, Miranda asked if she could have the table. "Go right ahead," I told her good-naturedly. "Feel free." She'd already taken the husband I no longer wanted; what did I care if she took a trestle table with scuffed-up legs and deep scratches that marked the place where Rick had dropped a piece of track lighting on it years earlier? The truth is, I wished them well. The two of us had married immediately after college, young and slightly stupid and crazy in love with each other. My mother was never thrilled with Rick, whom she described, then and now, as "a pessimist from the word 'go.'" She counseled me not to marry him, but why would I have listened? I was twenty-one years old, happier than I'd ever been, and not inclined to take the loving advice that had been offered me. "He'll drag you down with him," my mother warned. "And I pray I'm wrong even though I know I'm right."

She *was* right, but that's another story.

My son, Jesse, who is seventeen now, refused to attend Rick and Miranda's wedding. When the invitation came for him in the mail nearly two years ago, he took the little cream-colored card that said, "Please reply by June the first," and wrote, very neatly, "When hell freezes over, I might." I pointed out that this was childish—not to mention selfish—but all he could say was, "*Someone's* being childish and selfish and it isn't me."

Sometimes he's quite a bit smarter than I give him credit for.

The afternoon of the wedding, a glorious summer day, of course, the two of us went to a multiplex theatre near Lincoln Center and saw a couple of movies, one a pallid comedy with Sandra Bullock, the other some disappointing crime/thriller thing with Robert DeNiro. Emerging from the theatre four hours later, a bit dazed, we saw that the city had turned dark and glittery, and that this lousy day would soon come to a close. Rick and Miranda were now officially man and wife, which was perfectly all right with me. Frankly, at this stage of the game, Rick was no prize—his hair was thinning and wild, his posture was stooped, he made harsh snorting sounds as he slept at night and was generally his usual downbeat self.

If Miranda wanted him, honestly, she could have him. Though God knows what she saw in him. He was a corporate lawyer who made a pretty hefty salary, maybe that was it. Even so, couldn't she have set her sights on a younger guy, some hotshot attorney in his thirties with a spring to his step and a thousand-watt smile for each and every one of his clients and for the rest of the world as well?

Apparently not.

The wedding card I sent them showed a three-tiered cake trimmed in pink and white roses; inside were the words, "May the Joys of Your Wedding Day Last a Lifetime." I signed my name and Jesse's too, since he, big surprise, adamantly refused to add his signature.

"Try and get over it," I advised my son. "He may not be perfect but he's the only dad you get."

Jesse snorted when he heard this, sounding just like his father in the middle of the night.

After the DeNiro flick, we went straight to our favorite Szechuan restaurant at Broadway and 95th. But the pancakes that came with the moo shu beef were thick and starchy that night, and the glazed walnuts in the chicken dish had a bitter aftertaste. We never went back again, even though there was no place we liked better. Our family had a long history at Tang Tung's; we'd celebrated Jesse's first birthday there, with Jesse in his Sassy Seat that clipped onto the edge of the Formica table, using his chopsticks to beat out a baby song against a row of water glasses. Rick had been a second-year associate at the firm then, had just come off some crazy, nightmarish twenty-four-hour assignment, and had fallen asleep at the table, a pointed paper party hat strapped to his head with a rubber band.

This was long ago, before iPhones and iPods; Miranda herself was still in high school, where she was president of the Spanish Honor Society, junior editor of the yearbook, and possibly still a virgin.

Imagine that.

The instant I arrive home from work today, just as I'm walking through the door, the phone begins to ring.

"Got a minute?" Rick whispers.

"I can hardly hear you," I complain, and throw myself down onto the living-room couch.

"I'm on my cell phone in my therapist's waiting room. He had an emergency and he's running late," Rick says.

So he's seeing a shrink. This is the first I've heard of it and for some reason I find the news rather satisfying and actually smack my lips, as if I'd tasted something delicious.

"So what are you seeing a shrink for?" I ask, trying not to sound too interested.

"Where is it written that I have to tell you every last detail?" Rick says irritably.

I'm up out of my seat and in the kitchen now, pawing through the freezer in search of something microwavable for dinner. From down the hall I hear music, Eric Clapton crooning *Layla*. I'm not stupid: I know that Jesse and his girlfriend are having sex back there in his bedroom and that this is something that has been going on for months. They're both high school seniors, and openly lovey-dovey in my presence. And it's none of my business, though if I were Patti's mother I'd probably *make* it my business.

Taking note of a couple of Uncle Ben's Rice Bowl dinners in the freezer, I try not to contemplate the obvious, that while my son and my ex are both doing quite nicely in the romance department these days, I, the glue that held this family together for so long, have been left out in the cold. I'm no smokin' hot babe; there are little pillows of fat above my knees and the faint beginnings of bags under my eyes, but even though I wouldn't be caught dead in a bikini, I'm still a size six and proud of it. At least once a day I try and remind myself that just because I'm on the wrong side of forty doesn't mean my life is over.

"Look, I know you called to tell me *something*," I remind

Rick. Cordless phone in hand, I make my way down the hall with extreme caution, on silent tiptoes, and press my ear against Jesse's door. Now I hear Joni Mitchell's high-pitched keening and feel the sharp sting of something like grief pass swiftly through me. "What *is* it?" I whisper into the phone. It's been a couple of months since Miranda's lumpectomy and she's started her radiation treatments. The tumor was remarkably small, detected early, and her chances for a full recovery and a long life are excellent. I've heard this from Rick a good half-dozen times, as if I were the one who needed convincing.

"Could you possibly come over and check on Mandy?" he says at last. "I'm going to be a couple of hours late getting home tonight and she sounded really down today. I'm worried about her," he adds needlessly.

Interesting—of all the people in the world, I'm the one he has to call for this mission of mercy? "Doesn't she have any friends you can ask?" I say.

"She's got a load of friends," Rick assures me. "But they've all got babies or little kids to take care of or boyfriends or whatever. And besides, you're the one person I can always trust to do things right." He pauses. "You're a good soul, Carol," he says in a whisper, as if this were classified information not to be given out to just anyone.

A good soul? What am I, some ancient guru, some Gandhi or Albert Schweitzer in a rocking chair radiating goodness and wisdom to legions of the faithful?

"A *phenomenally* good soul," my ex says, laying it on thick.

"Oh, all right," I say with a sigh.

"So I can call and tell Miranda you're coming over?"

"You can call her."

"I could just hug you, you're so sweet," Rick says. "I could put my arms around you, and so on and so forth…"

"All right," I say. "E-nough."

"I'm so grateful to you for this."

"Yeah yeah, fine," I say, but secretly I'm pleased.

Before leaving for the Upper West Side, I slip a note under Jesse's door alerting him to the Rice Bowl dinners in the freezer—one for him and one for Patti, if they so desire. If not, they're on their own. I try to be a good mother, but who knows? Maybe a truly good mother would have flung open the bedroom door after a perfunctory knock and shrieked, "How dare you two have sex in my house right under my very nose! Shame on you both!"

It's not my style, but maybe it ought to be.

I catch a crowded crosstown bus at 86th Street and am forced to stand the whole way through the Park. After what feels like a too-long day at the office I'm more than a little tired, and I look hungrily at a seat occupied by a tiny boy with spiky red hair, no older than four or five, who should, by all rights, be stationed in his father's lap and not taking up valuable real estate like that.

"What's a buck?" the kid says to his father, who is deeply, passionately engrossed in a magazine, reading an article about the joys of dim sum. Canting my neck at just the right angle, I too can read about steamed bao dze and crabmeat stuffed in green spinach dough.

The father's not going to take his eyes from the magazine—it's just not worth the effort. "What?" he says. "Oh, it's a male deer."

"A buck is money, it's not an animal," the little boy says contemptuously.

"Okay, one buck equals one dollar, okay, Stevie? Why can't you sit quietly and stare out the window or something, huh?"

"That magazine is stupid and so are you," Stevie observes.

"Whatever," the father says. "Whatever you want."

Stevie is silent for a moment or two, and then he announces, matter-of-factly, "I'm thinking of stabbing you in the penis, Daddy."

This sounds to me like a good idea, and I smile at the little boy approvingly and then get out at my stop, thinking, well, at least I was never *that* kind of parent, so seduced by thoughts of dim sum that I couldn't be bothered engaging in meaningful conversation with my own child for a big two minutes.

An icy wind blows directly in my face as I walk a couple of blocks up Broadway in the dark. The thin jacket I'm wearing was a miscalculation, plus I've forgotten my gloves, and I blame both of these mistakes on Jesse, who's entitled to have sex with his girlfriend, I suppose, but not in his bedroom when he knew damn well I'd be home from work any minute. I ought to plan on a friendly little chat with him later, one that will include the words "inappropriate" and "punctilious" and "utter lack of consideration." The truth is, even the *thought* of such a talk adds to my weariness in a big way.

Miranda comes to the door barefoot and greets me with the faintest of smiles. She's dressed in drawstring pajama bottoms and a faded, watery-pink tank top; her strawberry-blonde hair is in a sloppy ponytail, and without her usual makeup she's alarmingly pale. Though still, it must be said, young and pretty.

"How *are* you, honey?" I say. My eyes fill, surprising me. Even though my marriage was well on its way down the tubes when Rick started seeing her, finding out about the two of them didn't exactly do wonders for my ego. But that's all ancient history now, really, and if Miranda needs a little cheering up, who's to say I'm not the guy for the job?

"How *am* I?" Miranda shoots me a woeful look. We walk up two steps to the foyer, and then into the living room with its fourteen-foot ceilings ornamented with beautifully carved dark wood beams. What I wouldn't give for an apartment like this, an apartment so spacious it's like a beautiful old house. But I'm the one who's the picture of health, and if my own apartment is cramped and charmless, so what? "How the hell do you *think* I am?" Miranda is saying.

"Well, you really don't look too bad," I say, "all things considered."

"Yeah, sure," Miranda says. She stretches out now on a silk-covered antique couch that doesn't look the least bit inviting.

I wait for her to offer me a place to sit, and when she doesn't, I help myself to a cushioned window seat and pull my legs up under me, giving the false impression that I'm as cozy and comfortable as if I were lounging around in my own home. "Well, you do look as if you've been through something," I concede. "But you're a beautiful girl, pretty enough to be a model, for God's sake."

Miranda's face is half-hidden in the crook of her folded arm. "I can't even wear a bra anymore," she reports grimly.

"Hmm?"

"Radiation five days a week for seven weeks, you know what that does to you?"

Lucky for me I don't. "Is it painful?" I say. I stare upward at those spectacular mahogany beams.

"It burned my skin," says Miranda, bursting into tears. "And that's why I can't wear a bra."

"Please don't cry," I say. I hop down from the window seat and collapse on the floor next to her, close enough to stroke her hair, her smooth, bony shoulder, the perfect curve of her jaw. I don't, though; something tells me to keep my distance. "How about if I make you a cup of tea or something?"

"I have a drawer full of bras from Victoria's Secret and I can't wear a single one of them because it hurts too much."

"Well," I say, "I'm sure that's only temporary."

"If I die, you can have them all," Miranda says generously. "Even the zebra print that's Rick's favorite."

I'm not interested in hearing about Rick's favorite anything, and would love to tell her so. "You're not going to die," I tell her instead. "That's bullshit and you know it."

"It's cancer, that's all *I* know."

"It was the tiniest tumor and now it's gone," I remind her. I'm beginning to lose my patience, which, under the circumstances, seems unforgivable, of course. I want to go home: a hot bath and a movie from Netflix would be lovely, I'm think-ing guiltily, and also an order of country-fried chicken salad in cracked-peppercorn parmesan dressing from that café on the corner of Second Avenue that always delivers in a jiffy. So this is the kind of woman I am, a woman who loses patience with a thirty-four-year-old cancer victim and fantasizes about that first mouthful of exceptionally crispy fried chicken salad and the warm fluffy biscuit that comes with it.

"You could make me soup," I hear Miranda saying. "Lipton's chicken noodle. And a brie sandwich on focaccia. And maybe some white peach iced tea, okay?"

"You bet," I say, and I'm already on my feet, racing through the living room and the parlor and the dining room, and then three steps up into the kitchen, propelled there by an odd, queasy mixture of guilt and relief.

Putting myself to work in the kitchen, I cut the tip of my finger on a bread knife. It serves me right, and don't I know it.

"Here's the dinner you ordered, ma'am," I say to Miranda in my cheeriest voice, but she looks at it with little interest.

"I can't," she tells me.

"Sure you can," I say. "We don't want the soup to get cold, do we?"

"I'm so tired I can barely lift my head," says Miranda. "It's the radiation, you know—I've only had the first four weeks, but it's cumulative; every day I'm a little more tired than the day before."

"You poor thing," I sigh, and go into the dark, high-ceilinged bedroom where Miranda and my ex have, no doubt, made love a thousand and one times. I grab the comforter off the bed, star-tled by the sight of Rick's maroon-and-white tattersall pajamas, which I bought for him maybe four or five years ago, when buy-ing him things—even something as ordinary as Ralph Lauren pajamas on sale for half-price—still gave me a little frisson of pleasure. The top button is missing, I notice, and the one in the middle is hanging by a thread. I bite it off with my teeth and slip it into the back pocket of my jeans, as if it might prove useful one day.

Miranda is asleep when I return to the living room. I arrange the comforter gently around her long, lean figure, and then I get busy on her sandwich.

No sense letting a perfectly good meal go to waste.

Leaning against the kitchen counter, I smoke a cigarette for dessert. Afterward, I rinse off the few things that are in the sink and load them into the dishwasher. There's a door that leads out from the kitchen to a small terrace, and even though you'd have to be crazy to go out there coatless on an ice-cold February night, that's precisely what I do, hugging myself fiercely as I catch sight of a star or two and a platinum half-moon. I think of Rick in his plaid pajamas kissing my perfumed throat as I slid my hand under his waistband and made a playful grab for him. It isn't that I miss him or the time when we approached one another so eagerly; it's only that we spent a lifetime together and what has it all come to? A stolen sliver of a button in my back pocket. A cold ache that settled in my chest and never seemed to go away, not even on the very best days. We were a dismal failure together, a total washout, and I can't get that out of my thick head, no matter how hard I try. Though maybe I just haven't been trying hard enough.

The kitchen door swings open; Rick steps out onto the terrace and asks me if I'm insane. "It's thirty degrees out here," he says. "I've already got one sick wife, what are you trying to do, make it two for two?" Draping his overcoat across my shoulders, he says, "How long has she been sleeping?"

"Not long, fifteen, twenty minutes, I guess." I turn the soft collar of his coat up against my neck. The collar smells like Obsession, the cologne I'd got into the habit of buying him for Christmas years ago. Apparently Miranda's been buying it too.

"I think she's in a clinical depression," Rick says. "You can't believe how depressing that is for me."

"For you?" I say, incensed. "For *you*?" And then I remind

myself that there's no point in getting all worked up over this. Any way you look at it, it's none of my business and never will be.

Rick loops his arm around my waist. "Don't be angry at me, Carol," he says. "Sometimes I'm just a big selfish baby."

We stand like that in the cold for a couple of minutes, not saying a word. Shutting my eyes, I lean my head against Rick's shoulder and listen to the familiar whoosh of traffic three stories below. "If you do, girl, I'll cut your eyes out and give them to a blind man!" a voice threatens cheerfully from somewhere beyond us. And then we go back inside and I fix my ex a sandwich, the same one I'd made for Miranda but on an ordinary poppy-seed roll that is noticeably stale but the only thing I can find. I feel guilty for this, too, and also for having rested my head lazily against Rick's shoulder in a moment of pure weakness. Or maybe weariness. Honestly, I ought to move out of this city and away from here, away from these two troubled souls who need looking after but not by me.

"Cambridge, Massachusetts," I say.

"What about it?" Rick says. His face looks long and drawn, and he really could use a haircut, at the very least a trim.

"Nothing. I'm thinking of moving there, that's all," I tell him. "And if you've got a good pair of scissors, I could trim your hair for you."

"Why?" he says.

"It's not a flattering style," I say. "In fact, it's no style at all. Truthfully, you look a little grungy."

"I meant why are you thinking of moving back to Cambridge? Of course we were really happy there, all those years ago."

"It's just a thought I've been kicking around," I say. "And for the record, *you* weren't the one who was happy there. You were in law school and you were miserable."

"We were happy *together*," Rick insists. "Don't deny it."

"You're right," I admit, remembering a lot of leisurely

sex, most of it in the middle of one long Saturday afternoon or another. And the two of us hanging out at Harvard Square every weekend, lingering in bookstores and used record stores with countless other twenty-somethings, so young and energetic we couldn't imagine a time when we'd be middle-aged and wilting and heartsick.

"You're not really serious about moving away, are you?" Rick says.

"Well, I might be," I say, and shrug one shoulder.

"Like I have any right to try and stop you," my ex says wistfully.

"Just get me a pair of scissors. And some newspaper."

In the living room, Miranda lets out a noisy sigh or yawn; it's hard to tell from this distance.

"Why don't you go and see how she's doing?" I urge Rick.

"What about my haircut?"

"First things first!" I order. "Jesus!" How has it come to pass that I'm the one calling the shots here?

"Aren't you coming with me?"

My lips pursed, I shake my head slowly from side to side, as if Rick were some exasperating child who just won't listen. "The only place I'm going is home," I say.

But first, out of consideration for Miranda and her life-threatening illness, I tidy up their beautiful, expensive kitchen, all imported granite and stainless steel, the likes of which wouldn't be out of place in *Architectural Digest*. Not that I'm the least bit envious; why would I be? My own kitchen has plastic cabinets and a chipped linoleum-tile floor, but so what? As they used to say in that insipid commercial that was on TV every other minute in the Seventies, or maybe it was the Eighties, *If you've got your health, you've got everything*. And don't I know it.

There's another sinkful of dishes waiting for me at home. Unbelievable. It seems the love of my son's life made angel hair in olive oil and garlic and threw in a load of red, green, and yellow peppers. They abandoned the leftovers on top of the stove in plain view, without even a thought to a sheet of Saran Wrap. Patti herself is nowhere to be found and Jesse is in his room, slumped at his desk with earbuds in his ears, a book of Anne Sexton's poems open in front of him. And just to keep himself busy, his hands are playing with a plastic Slinky.

"Hey," he says when I tap him on the shoulder.

I point to his earbuds and he slips them out obligingly. "Interesting reading?" I say.

"Man, that Anne Sexton was one fucked-up chick," he says. "You can't believe what went on in that family."

"Be that as it may, I'm not in the mood to clean up that mess you and Patti left in the kitchen. I've cleaned up enough kitchens for one day." I tell him where I've been and he scowls at me. He's a handsome kid in a Grateful Dead T-shirt that says, "36,086 SONGS, 2,317 CONCERTS, 298 CITIES, 1 BAND." Jesse would be the first to deny it, but he's a little too skinny and his hair is way too short, thanks to the neighborhood barber who just didn't know when to call it quits. Like his father, Jesse is prone to moods of the bleakest sort, and his bedroom door is almost always closed. But he's not a druggy—and least not that I know of—and his grades have always been in the A-/B+ range. So who am I to complain?

"No offense," he says, "but you're kind of a loser for going over there. You shouldn't have anything to do with them."

"She's sick," I say defensively. "She had cancer surgery."

"Obviously that's very sad," Jesse says, "but what's that got to do with *you?*"

"Well, nothing, really," I say. I feel my face blazing, as if I've been deeply humiliated. "Your father asked me to do him a favor and I did it. End of story."

Jesse rolls his eyes. "Yeah right," he says. "What *you* need," he informs me, "is to get your shit together and just say no the next time he asks."

"There's not going to be a next time, okay? I have better things to do, believe me," I say. I begin compiling a list in my head, in case he happens to ask for one. It's not a long list, but it's long enough…there are novels piled up on the coffee table I'm desperate to read, concerts at Lincoln Center I want to go to, an exhibit at the Whitney I've been meaning to get to for a month now, movies I'm willing to shell out fourteen bucks to see, an exercise class at the Y up the block that meets two nights a week…surely I can keep myself busy in the greatest city in the world, can't I?

Jesse tosses me his Slinky. "Good catch," he says.

"I'm far from stupid," I announce. "You don't have to worry about me." And then I allow myself a good look at his bed, a sight I've been avoiding ever since I set foot in the room. A couple of pillows are squashed into one corner and the dingy black-and-white comforter is carelessly peeled almost all the way back, exposing a rumpled-looking pale blue sheet. "I hope to God you're using condoms," I hear myself say, and pitch the Slinky straight to him.

There's a long, miserable silence during which I examine the tips of my boots, which, I notice, could use a polishing.

"Please get out of my room," Jesse says finally.

"I just need to know that you're being careful," I say, sounding apologetic.

"Out!" my son bellows, which isn't like him.

I'm already over the threshold and out in the hallway. "You want the door open or shut?" I squeak.

From his seat at the desk, he reaches out and whams the door shut behind me, so hard the walls actually vibrate.

The next time Rick calls, a few weeks later, I'm ready with a list of excuses as long as my arm. Dispensing with all pleasantries, he gets down to business immediately. He tells me he's on a case that's going to take him out of town for a few days and that he'd be grateful if I'd look in on Miranda while he's away. "*Really* grateful," he says, "believe me."

"I'm sorry," I say, and take a deep, cowardly breath. "I just can't." It's a Saturday afternoon and I'm killing time watching a movie about five blonde teenage sisters with a thirst for suicide. The youngest has just jumped to her death and the rest will be goners by the end of the movie. One down, four to go. I know this because I've read the book, which wasn't as depressing as you'd think. "I just can't," I repeat, suddenly unable to remember a single one of my excuses.

Rick sighs heavily into the phone. "I've got an incredibly high level of anxiety in my life right now," he says.

"What else is new?" I say, pausing the DVD so I can devote my full attention to the matter at hand.

"My therapist says I've got to take steps to reduce that anxiety or I'm going to crash."

"What's that supposed to mean?" I say suspiciously.

"Well, it means I've got to put some distance between myself and the source of that anxiety."

I've heard about as much psychobabble as I can take. "Speak English," I say, "or I'm hanging up."

"Wanna have lunch?" Rick asks.

"With you?" I say. "I doubt it. And besides, it's after four. Lunch came and went a couple of hours ago."

"Let's have coffee, then."

"Do I drink coffee? We were married for a thousand years and you still don't know the answer to that question?"

"Oh, right, you're the Diet Coke queen," Rick says fondly.

"Where's Miranda?" I say.

"Sleeping sleeping sleeping. It's all she ever does these days—that, and drag herself out of the house for an occasional manicure and a facial."

I hear the microwave being slammed shut; Jesse is finally up and about. The kid has barely spoken to me since that night I so unwisely used the word "condoms" in a simple, well-meaning sentence. If he doesn't snap out of it soon and start acting like a decent human being in my presence, I'm going to pack his bags and send him over to his father's, where the two of them can sulk to their hearts' content. You know what: I've had it up to here with them both. *Had* it.

"So how about it, can I treat you to a Diet Coke?" Rick is saying.

What the hell; at least it will get me up and out of the apartment. "I'll see you at the Black Sheep in half an hour. And be prepared for a lecture or two," I warn.

"What, I'm afraid of you?" Rick says, and laughs.

I change into my best black jeans and a thin wool turtleneck that's always been a little too tight across the chest, though it's soft and clean and a beautiful shade of pale gray. In the bathroom I wet down my hair, shake it out, work in some expensive gel. I gloss my lips with something bronze, pinch my cheeks viciously for a bit of color. On my way out of the bathroom I bump into Jesse, who nods, and murmurs, "Hey." He's in a T-shirt and boxers, and his beautiful dark eyes look dull and bleary, as if ten hours of sleep haven't done him an ounce of good.

"Oh, for Christ's sake!" I cry impulsively, and fold my arms around the sharp wings of his shoulder blades. "You can't imagine how much I love you."

"It's not that I don't love you," my son tells me, "it's just that you're so annoying."

"Define 'annoying,'" I say as his arms slowly rise and circle my back tentatively.

"You think you're in charge of everything," Jesse says. "But you can't be, okay? Get that through your head and we'll be fine."

"We will?"

Jesse shrugs and lets go of me. "Gotta pee," he says. "Catch you later."

In the elevator, on my way down to the lobby, the only other passenger on board is an ancient old woman in a puffy down coat accessorized with a leopard-skin purse. She stares at me relentlessly.

"Hello," I say, hoping that will be enough.

"I did not do my zipper," she says. "Please?" The woman takes off her coat and hands it to me, then turns her back. "Zip up?" she says.

"No problem." Without hesitation, I place my fingers at the base of her spine and zip up her dress just as we arrive at the lobby.

The elevator door slides open, but she stays where she is, peering inside her leopard-skin purse now. "Thank you, nice lady," she says, and offers me a dollar.

"No!" I say. "No no no. And here, let me help you with your coat."

"No no no?"

"Absolutely not," I say, mortified. Inexplicably, I've sweat through my turtleneck.

"Goodbye, lady," the woman says, waving the dollar bill in farewell as I fly from the elevator and through the lobby and out into the street. It takes me a while to catch my breath; honestly, I don't know what's wrong with me.

Here's my secret: occasionally it's my son I rely on to zip me all the way up, to fiddle with a particularly tricky clasp on a necklace or bracelet for me, to deftly remove an unruly DVD stuck in the player in our living room. So what will I do when, as planned, he goes off to college next fall? Solicit help from fellow passengers in the elevator, bow my bare neck low so a stranger's hands can hook my pearls for me?

With my head lifted high, my back straight as a soldier's, I walk the three short blocks to meet my ex. Of course he's not there yet and of course they won't seat me without him.

I prefer to wait outside in the cold, where a couple of

pigeons are enjoying a take-out meal, pecking at the remains of a foil-wrapped taco. A little girl in a stroller rolls by, chatting on a cell phone. His chin propped up in his palm, a man with a shaved head leans disconsolately against a parking meter. "Holy smoke," he says darkly.

As usual, I've forgotten my gloves, and I stick my hands into the pockets of my leather jacket, pissed off at Rick for making me wait for him. Who, after all, invited whom for a drink?

When his cab pulls up, finally, and he tumbles out, full of apologies, I just don't want to hear it. "And don't kiss me like that," I complain as his lips brush hurriedly against my cheek.

"Don't kiss you?" he says, surprised and insulted.

"Just don't."

The Black Sheep is filled with customers at this odd hour between lunch and dinner, and the waitress seats us at a table uncomfortably close to the restroom.

"Switch seats with me," I tell Rick. Why not let *him* be the one to watch the bathroom door swing open every few minutes?

"Fine." His hair, I notice, is still kind of a mess, and pushed back so that it exposes his small, delicate ears.

"You still need a haircut," I say after I order my Diet Coke and a dessert called Death by Chocolate.

"Nice sweater," he observes.

Instinctively, I cross my arms over my chest.

Rick sips at a glass of water with a slice of lemon floating on top. "My therapist thinks I ought to…" he says, but I'm not listening. Not to a sentence that begins with the words, "My therapist thinks."

At the table adjacent to ours a woman says, "My mother really did love you, you know."

"Oh, I'm sure she did, in her own sick way," her companion says. "I believe it."

"So that's that," Rick is saying.

"I'm sorry, did I miss something?"

"Yeah, it's just that my therapist thinks it might do my

marriage some good if I spent a little time away from Miranda for a while, nothing permanent, but kind of like a vacation from each other," my ex says, so casually that it makes my blood boil. "And I figured you'd want to know."

I lean across the table and grab him by the wrist. "*What*? You can't be serious," I say. I think of Miranda's burned, tender skin, the pallor of her face, her offer to bequeath every last one of her sexy bras from Victoria's Secret to me. According to my calculations, she's got one more week of radiation left and then she's home free.

"Where's your compassion?" I ask, outraged. "What about that whole 'in sickness and in health' deal, huh?"

"Please let go of my wrist."

"Not until you promise to at least reconsider this…this so-called vacation of yours," I say, and dig my thumbnail into his flesh.

Yanking his hand away, Rick says, "I don't get it. What's it to you, anyway?"

My Death by Chocolate has arrived, a pitch-dark wedge marinating in hot fudge, and Rick's got his eye on it. "What's it to me?" I say. "It hurts me to see you acting like such a bastard, that's all."

"You really think I'm a bastard?" he says in astonishment. "Don't you think it kills me that I'm incapable of being the person I should be, that I *want* to be?" The tips of his ears have turned crimson, and I have an urge to reach across the Formica between us and feel their heat. I can't help myself: effortlessly, I remember him as a brand-new father, ferrying Jesse around in a denim pouch against his chest, his face lowered to nuzzle the top of the baby's fluffy-haired, still-soft head. You don't forget things like that; you allow them to haunt you occasionally, to remind you that it wasn't merely one disappointment after another, and that, from time to time, things were just right.

"Get your fork out of my dessert, please," I say. "And go home to your wife."

"Even when you're angry at me," Rick says, fork poised in the air, "there's still stuff about you that I find kind of alluring."

My palms are like ice, and damp with sweat. Rick shows me what I've done to the underside of his wrist, where tiny scarlet beads of blood have appeared all in a row. Raising his hand to my lips, I savor the taste of salt, but only for an instant.

"Go home to your wife," I repeat. "Scram." Something in my voice lets him know that I mean business; he's already out of his seat now, fumbling with his coat.

"If only I could make you understand how it feels not to be able to do anything right anymore," Rick says softly, and, making his way to the door without even a goodbye, sticks me with the bill.

There's a decrepit old Chevy Citation parked in front of my building, I see as I head homeward—a rusting piece of junk with a tinted windshield and a bumper sticker that announces:

I STILL MISS MY EX BUT MY AIM IS IMPROVING

I can't resist: I give the rear bumper a good swift kick, the kind that sets the tips of my toes tingling with something that's not exactly pain but close enough. My hands are in the back pockets of my jeans now, and I go straight for that pajama button, which, though worthless, is one hundred percent mine.

TODAY IS NOT YOUR DAY

THE UNIFORMED EMTs, a pair of forty-something blondes friendly as can be, arrive only six minutes after her fall, before she has felt even the faintest pinch of pain, despite the fact that her knee cap seems to have vanished. Rolling onto her side, staring upward at the coolly modern, glass-and-steel light fixture on the ceiling in the narrow hallway of her apartment, Lauren pretends that everything that has gone wrong today is about to be righted.

Yeah, good luck with that.

At her side, Alex, her onetime fiancé, hovers, iPhone in hand. He is big-boned, six feet four inches tall, but still must watch his weight, which he does, vigilantly. He sells security systems to large companies in the US and abroad, and makes more money in a year than Lauren, a caseworker for the homeless in Manhattan, will probably see in five.

So be it, as her mother liked to say.

The EMTs, who are named Barbara and Shianne, squat beside Lauren, asking how she happened to find herself on the floor, and praising her for having been smart enough not to try to move from where she'd fallen. "Such a dumb thing," Lauren acknowledges, wincing as she offers her quick little synopsis: polished floor, heels on her favorite black leather boots dangerously worn down, she herself racing along the slightly slippery hallway, needing one of her Marlboro Lights before running out to dinner with Alex.

She won't, in fact, be eating dinner of any sort at all until Tuesday. And today is only Sunday, the day, she will soon learn, that her patella shattered into five pieces the moment she hit the floor. And also the day that, just minutes ago, Alex broke the news to her—like a fierce bolt of lightning from the clearest of skies—that he was having second and third thoughts about their recent engagement.

The two of them were standing in their narrow kitchen, facing each other as Lauren leaned her elbows against the counter; she could see the constellation of fingerprints on the stainless steel refrigerator and thought of taking a few steps forward and wiping them off with a paper towel.

Oh, and to be entirely honest, Alex went on, he'd decided that, given those disturbing thoughts of his, it would be best if he *withdrew* (and here he'd coiled his hand into a fist and coughed into it) *from the, um, relationship.*

Withdrew?

People withdrew money from their checking accounts at the ATM, they withdrew from the world, perhaps, but they didn't withdraw from their fiancées. They broke up with them and left them reeling.

But obviously, Alex added, Lauren should feel free to keep the ring, a slightly flawed one-carat diamond that had belonged to his long-deceased great-grandmother, Elsie. And of course he and Lauren could still have one last dinner out together, if that's what she wanted, he told her.

"You're kidding, right?" Lauren said. "Very funny. I mean, hilarious," she continued, smiling in confusion. And her heart began to tick faster than usual.

"*Not* kidding," Alex said. He sighed, jutting his lower lip forward unattractively, though he was, certainly, an attractive guy—square-jawed, straight-nosed, hazel-eyed. "Not kidding, and really, really sorry," he told Lauren. "As sorry as I can be."

"Are you on drugs?" she said. "Have you been talking to Keith again?" Keith was one of his old friends from grad school who liked to drink on the weekends until he passed out. And who also had something of a coke habit. Like Alex, he had an MBA from Harvard, but he was still, in Lauren's opinion, kind of an idiot.

Alex shook his head. "*Definitely* not on drugs. And haven't spoken to Keith in a couple of months."

"So wait, can you please tell me what these second thoughts are?" Lauren managed to say. The inside of her mouth felt sandy, and when she tried to swallow, it was as if her throat had closed up.

"You know," Alex said vaguely.

No, she *didn't* know, but she planned to find out every last mortifying detail. Just as soon as she got her pack of Marlboro Lights from the bedroom the two of them shared.

"Uh-huh, uh-huh, just a simple slip 'n' fall," Shianne—who seems to be in charge—is saying now. She slides her fingertips into the empty cavity formerly occupied by Lauren's patella, and announces that, with any luck, it may turn out that the knee itself is only dislocated.

"So maybe you'll be lucky today," Alex says, on his own knees now beside Lauren. "Wouldn't it be great if it was just a dislocation?"

"Fuck you," she tells him through clenched teeth, though she's never spoken to him this way in the nearly four years they've been together. "Like you *give* a crap," she says for good measure. The EMTs show no sign of having heard her, though it's impossible that they missed those half-dozen little words. They've probably heard plenty worse, Lauren thinks, and anyway, it's none of their business *what* she says to Alex. Or why.

"Hey, do you guys have scissors I can use?" Shianne asks. "I need to cut your pants, Lauren, so we can get a better look at this knee of yours."

But these are Lauren's favorite pants, designer jeans plucked from the racks of Second Chance, one of those stores full of formerly pricey, "gently used" merchandise; visiting her neighborhood tailor a few years ago, Lauren had these particular jeans shortened to fit her flawlessly. And there's no way in hell she's going to let this kind, well-meaning EMT destroy them.

"Sorry, but believe it or not, we don't," she says.

"Don't be ridiculous," Alex says. He immediately goes off to get the scissors they keep in the ceramic mug that rests on the kitchen counter.

It's Barbara's brilliantly simple idea that Shianne cut along the seam so that Lauren can return the pants to the tailor for a quick fix sometime soon; even so, the sight of those all-purpose, blue-handled steel scissors clicking their way up the leg of her beloved jeans upsets Lauren more than it should.

Now she's being lifted onto a stretcher and wheeled to the elevator and through the lobby of the high-rise where she and Alex have lived so happily, so cozily, these past couple of years since they both turned thirty, first Lauren and then Alex, their birthdays only a few months apart.

In the lobby, the doorman and the concierge on duty wave goodbye and wish her a speedy recovery, then turn their attention to the delivery girl from Get Reel Videos, who, unaccountably, has arrived carrying a pizza.

It occurs to Lauren that this one-bedroom condo of Alex's legally belongs only to him, and that, quite possibly, she's in imminent danger of becoming homeless. Not unlike the clients whose lives she works so hard—and often, so fruitlessly—to improve. (Fruitlessly, she's discovered, because not everyone who desperately needs help actually wants it.)

She tries to bar Alex from the ambulance, but he insists

he wouldn't dream of leaving her alone (*Oh really?* she thinks), insists on accompanying her on the half-mile trip to the hospital. When, in the ambulance, he takes her hand and pats it, Lauren tells him that he's gone too far. For someone who no longer loves her, she means. "Touch me again, and I'll blow you away," Lauren warns him. And this is when it hits her that today is December 7th, Pearl Harbor Day, commemorating that surprise military attack conducted more than a half century ago.

The ER doc is even blonder than the EMTs and smiles inappropriately as she interprets the X-rays for Lauren. "I see right here, and here and here and here and here, the five pieces of your messed-up patella," she says. "I mean messed up *big* time, but one of our surgeons will put it back together nicely for you, okay? You're scheduled for surgery sometime Monday morning, how's that?"

"Sweet!" Lauren says with enthusiasm, because this is what's expected of her. She's still reclining on the stretcher she was carried in on, with a dense pillow beneath her head and her eye make-up a little smeary, and though she's almost always warm, even in winter, she's feeling a chill now, and has to ask Alex to look for an extra blanket. She hopes never to have to ask him for anything ever again; even asking for something as insignificant as a hospital blanket makes her uneasy. If Alex no longer loves her—and evidently he doesn't—she just wants him to disappear from her life as swiftly and as cleanly as possible. At least that's what she's been telling herself. Repeatedly, ever since the moment when Alex assumed his new role as her ex.

He finds a thin white cotton blanket for her that looks and feels like a cheap bath towel.

"The nurse says they'll have a room ready for you upstairs in an hour or so," he reports, adjusting the blanket carefully at her waist.

"Go home," Lauren tells him. "If I start to feel lonely, I'll call my father to come and sit with me."

"Your father lives in Westchester. By the time he gets here, you'll be upstairs in your room."

Miraculously, Lauren's wrecked knee is still scarcely painful at all; she told the ER doc and the pair of nurses who've been checking on her that on a scale of one to ten—ten reflecting unbearable agony—her pain registers only an unimpressive two. Well, maybe three.

Everyone remarks on her good fortune; to be honest, one of the nurses confides, they were expecting to hear her shrieking for morphine.

Later, up on the orthopedics ward, a fourth-year med student, age twenty-five, stops by her bed and suggests, somewhat condescendingly, that Lauren is in shock, her mind refusing to accept her injury, this nasty affront to her body.

Oh, she's in shock all right. And hasn't yet been presented with even a scintilla of evidence of what she has or hasn't done to earn Alex's dissatisfaction, disapproval, disdain, you name it. She's been made redundant; isn't that what they call it in England when you've been sacked?

But the knee, at least, is fixable; a couple of hours in the O.R. on Monday morning, and Lauren will be good to go, the med student assures her. As for the rest of her life (the life which, a scant few hours ago, included Alex and his nicely appointed Upper West Side apartment—which Lauren helped decorate with those carefully chosen steel-framed reproductions of Pollock and Rothko prints, not to mention the industrial carpeting in the living room and the glass-topped dining table and black leather chairs surrounding it): well, if love and a comfortable place to live in Manhattan are no longer part of the equation, it seems she'll have no choice but to leave them behind and move on, never mind that placing one foot in front of the other and propelling herself up and out aren't in the realm of possibility for her at the moment. *And she doesn't yet know the half of it:* not a thing about the foam-padded, metal-hinged brace that will, post-op, extend from her ankle to her hip, immobilizing her knee for eight interminable weeks. Nor does she have more than an inkling of the mortifying assistance she'll need, once released from the hospital, in getting to and from the bathroom, into and out of the shower, even into and out of the bed she and Alex have shared for a couple of happy, mostly uneventful years together.

In all honesty, Lauren can't imagine where she might have gone wrong. And if she weren't currently confined to a hospital bed, facing a two-hour surgery and God knows what else on Monday morning, she'd press Alex to tell her right now why their engagement has come undone. And why so unceremoniously. But she just doesn't have the stomach for it now. Looking down at the brilliant-cut diamond on her stubby little ring finger, she contemplates yanking it off and flinging it in Alex's direction. But he's busy channel-surfing on the small flat-screen TV suspended above her bed, and the moment isn't quite right. Seriously, though, what *is* she going to do with the ring, she asks herself. It doesn't belong on her finger; the sight of it there makes her feel pathetic. Not to mention unloved and abandoned. How hard could it be to remove it from her finger and offer it back to Alex? She gives it a shot, but Great-grandma Elsie's ring seems to have a mind of its own and refuses to slide over the second joint of Lauren's finger no matter how vigorously she twists it. A squirt of liquid soap would take care of things, but even the thought of that ordinary effort drains her.

"Not much of a selection here," Alex complains. "No HBO, no Showtime, no Cinemax."

"Alex," Lauren says, "go home."

"You want me to leave?" He looks genuinely puzzled. Weekends, to keep in shape, he often rides twenty-five miles a day on his $3000 Schwinn, and Lauren has to admit that standing here now in his navy blue V-necked sweater and olive green corduroys, he looks fit and handsome, so much so that she wants to slug him.

"You better get out of here before I punch you," she advises.

And is startled when he recklessly drops a kiss on her forehead just before he leaves, promising to return tomorrow morning before her surgery, which has been scheduled for eleven a.m.

"Gimme a break and don't bother coming back," Lauren calls after him; she pretends that her roommate, the plumpish, middle-aged woman in the bed next to hers, can't hear her.

Why would she want this man, who has fallen out of love with her, to hold her hand tomorrow just before the surgeon takes a whack at her?

She doesn't start to weep until after Alex leaves and a plate of sickly yellow mac and cheese is delivered to her bedside table on an eggplant-colored tray, along with a mini-bowl of chicken broth, a sealed plastic cup of applesauce, and an individual-sized can of pineapple juice.

Her roommate, who evidently has rejected her hospital gown and is dressed in clothing from home—a lilac sweat suit and matching terry cloth slippers—asks if Lauren's planning to eat her applesauce.

"What? You can have the whole tray if you want," Lauren tells her.

But her roommate only wants the applesauce, and instructs her to toss it across the room to her. "I'm Serra," she says. "Not Sarah," she explains, and spells out her name for Lauren. She is, she soon volunteers, fifty-one years old with two ruined kidneys and a spot on the transplant waiting list—along with 80,000 other hopefuls—at the United Network for Organ Sharing. Even one good kidney would be a miraculous gift, she explains. Until a kidney is offered, however, she's forced to spend nearly four hours, three days a week, in dialysis. "In my spare time," she says, rolling her eyes, "I work thirty-five hours a week as a legal secretary, a job I can't afford to quit because the medical benefits are so good. I'm running on empty," she admits, and shrugs.

"I'm so sorry," Lauren murmurs.

"But why are *you* crying?" Serra asks. "And maybe I'll take some of your mac and cheese after all. But only if you're sure you don't want it."

"I'm positive," Lauren says, and then, quietly, "My fiancé dumped me today." She has two perfectly good kidneys and is, except for her knee, healthy as a horse, but, nonetheless, she can't resist feeling sorry for herself here in her hospital bed, too queasy to contemplate what it might be like to swallow down a small mouthful of glutinous-looking mac and cheese. Even this smallest touch of self-pity is a character flaw, she realizes, and feels so ashamed in the presence of poor, unlucky Serra that she actually blushes. Under her breath, and to make herself feel better, she curses Alex and his unaccountable failure to continue to love her. And then curses *herself* for not offering up one of her kidneys to Serra here and now.

Serra is out of bed and approaching Lauren's mac and cheese, brandishing a salad fork. "Hold on, he dumped you *today*? When you broke your, what, knee? What an asshole!"

This assessment seems accurate enough, though, in all fairness to Alex, Lauren tells her roommate, he did, in truth, dump her several minutes *before* she fell. And has never, that she can recall, shown himself to be anything other than a pretty good guy. (Except, perhaps, when she asked him to accompany her and her father to synagogue services the Friday evening after her mother's death. *The atheist in me just won't allow it*, Alex told her. *Not even to make you happy for an hour.* The two of them had sex in her childhood bedroom that night, while Lauren's bereft father slept in the room across the hall, and Alex did make her happy, though for somewhat less than an hour.)

"He's *not* a good guy, he's an asshole," Serra repeats. "You're lying to yourself, Lauren, whether you know it or not. It's just like with my brother and me. Until I asked him for a kidney, I would have described *him* as a good guy, too. My sister told me not to ask him, told me that he didn't want to offer me the kidney and that I absolutely shouldn't ask. But he's a potential match, so how could I not? I called him up because I was too chicken to ask in person, and when he said, 'Um, sorry, no can do, kiddo,' it hit me that nothing he could say or do in the future would ever repair the damage he did in that one single moment. Nothing! He wouldn't even agree to get tested. He's my brother, but, well, screw *him*." Tucking into Lauren's mac and cheese now, Serra says, "But the thing is, he's got a set of eight-year-old twins to take care of, and it was his wife who told him he had to say no. So...maybe I should stop being so angry, right?"

"I don't know what I..." Lauren begins, and then an Indian nurse with a maroon-colored bindi at the center of her brow arrives to check her blood pressure and Serra's; a few minutes later, another nurse appears, checks their IVs, and wishes them both a blessed night, which she pronounces "bless-ed."

"A bless-ed night to you, too," Serra says, but Lauren merely offers an utterly nonsectarian "thank you."

She feels thoroughly embarrassed the instant she awakens from her dismal dream. In it, she was wearing a wedding gown, a none-too-shabby Vera Wang (which, in real life, Lauren had admired in *Modern Bride*), and escorted by her father, made it halfway down the aisle, where Alex met her—dressed, oddly, in jeans and a sweat-drenched T-shirt. Drawing back Lauren's veil, Alex kissed her before the seated rows of smiling guests, then announced, in a booming voice Lauren never knew he possessed, that he felt it best to withdraw. *Withdraw from what? Are you insane?* her father said, echoing the guests, every one of whom looked clueless.

When the orderly comes to transport her to the O.R. at ten forty-five in the morning, Alex still hasn't shown up, though he does call to wish Lauren good luck. He claims to have been caught up in a lengthy conference call with a client in Mumbai, and even though Lauren doesn't believe him and his uninspired excuse, she finds herself grateful for his call.

"Right, thanks," she says. And then, to annoy the atheist in him, adds, "Oh yeah, and don't forget to have a bless-ed day."

———

So much for her simple, pain-free slip 'n' fall: awakening at precisely six o'clock the morning following her surgery, Lauren knows she needs something truly potent, a narcotic that will do the job and do it right. She squeezes the call button, and waits anxiously, staring as the large circle of a classroom-appropriate clock on the wall across from her bed reports that nearly ten minutes have passed. And she's still no closer to being pain-free than she was when she first pressed the button. On the other side of the room, Serra appears to be sleeping comfortably; even though Lauren knows it's senseless, she envies her. And tries the call button again. Another ten minutes pass, and, at last, a nurse appears. But in reality, she's a nurse's aide, and cannot help Lauren, as she is quick to communicate. "Your nurse is on her break," the woman says indifferently, "and I can't do anything for you."

"Please, I'll take *anything*," Lauren says. "Even just plain Tylenol with codeine, anything you have for me." She stretches out her arm and touches the woman's wrist. "Please."

The nurse's aide remains unmoved. She makes no attempt to soothe or sympathize; she just turns her back to Lauren and leaves the room. Lauren's reminded of a T-shirt she saw a guy wearing on the subway last summer:

I CAN ONLY BE NICE TO ONE PERSON A DAY AND TODAY IS NOT YOUR DAY

At seven o'clock, after she's finally given the Percocet she so richly deserves, she realizes she has to pee. The nurse's aide returns, draws the curtain around the bed, and helps Lauren onto the bedpan, none too delicately.

"I'll be back," she says.

"Please don't leave," Lauren says. "I'll be finished in a

minute, I promise."

"You do your business, and I'll do mine," the woman says. And vanishes.

Abandoned, still sitting on the bedpan eighteen minutes later, Lauren is near tears. She can't reach the call button to summon assistance without moving off the plastic basin fitted beneath her, and is stuck, mortifyingly, behind a curtain, unable to do anything but pray that help will be along soon enough. But it isn't, and so she makes what feels like a decision of real importance, and eases herself off the pan on her own, then gingerly lowers it to the floor beside her bed, careful not to swish any fluid over the top and onto the linoleum floor.

"What's this on the floor here?" the next nurse to saunter by asks. "What if I'd stepped into your mess and knocked it over, then what? Can't you be a little more CONSIDERATE?"

Lauren's knee is in pieces, tethered by loops of wire and metal hooks. Her leg continues to ache, no matter what drugs she swallows, and her face hasn't been washed since Sunday, which, she believes, was two days ago. And now she's been criticized for being inconsiderate. "My fiancé just broke up with me," she hears herself say, hoping for a smidgen of sympathy, hoping that there's not even a trace of whininess in her voice. But is there no end to her mortification? If her homeless, paranoid schizophrenic, drug- and alcohol-addicted clients could hear her now, they would laugh in her pained, sweaty face. *No offense, but what the fuck's wrong with you, Miss Lauren? You got to get yourself some dignity, baby!*

The nurse fails to be impressed by what Lauren knows to be her pathetic confession about Alex. "You look like you need a sponge bath," is all the woman offers.

"I do," Lauren agrees. "And a fresh nightgown, please." She has no desire to study herself in a mirror, knowing that what she will see is the face of someone in need of lipstick, mouthwash, a toothbrush adorned with a half-inch of Crest, Colgate, or Aquafresh, and, most important of all, a long, very hot shower—the longer and hotter the better. And after that, a few swipes under each arm with a stick of Soft & Dri. As much as she wants these things, the thought of attending to them, even lifting a toothbrush to her mouth, exhausts her. She who works ten-hour days along the Bowery, engaged in the hard, hard work of coaxing her clients off the street and into shelters and hospitals.

Face it: she's a mess. And one without a significant other. Though here's her father, visiting at lunchtime now, staying long enough to inform her that she looks terrible. *(Gee, thanks, Dad!)* And that the Belgian chocolate he's brought her costs twenty-eight dollars a pound. "Can you believe it?" he says. "For chocolate!" When he kisses Lauren goodbye, he says he'll be back tomorrow, and this time might even bring his girlfriend, even though all three of them know that Lauren's never been able to warm to her. (For the usual reasons—Roxanna's hair is dyed a strikingly unnatural shade of orangey-red; she talks too much and says too little; and, most annoying of all, has a sibilant "S" that drives Lauren crazy.)

"Roxanna really wants to come and see you, despite the fact that she's fully aware you don't like her," her father says.

"I do too like her," Lauren says now, but without much conviction.

"Honey, you don't," her father insists. "And Roxanna's fine with it. She understands how much you loved Mom. She wouldn't dream of trying to compete with a dead woman."

Lauren's father is a psych professor at NYU, but sometimes, she thinks, he seems bent on proving that he's not the sharpest crayon in the box. Or even the second sharpest.

As he talks, she lies silent, wiggling the toes of her bad leg (as the nurses call it, as if the leg itself has been disobedient), and imagining how lovely it would be to stand behind the glass door of the shower at home and let the steamy water run over every inch of her.

(Her surgeon will pop in for a cursory visit later in the

afternoon and let her know that there will be no showering for *the next fourteen days,* not until after the many stitches in her incision have been removed—a piece of news that will reduce Lauren to bitter tears. Over a shower, of all things! Because without her daily shower, she just isn't her real self, the one who runs with the homeless and does her best to significantly improve their sad, mean lives.)

"Give my love to Alex," her father says innocently, sailing out the door in his coffee-colored suede shoes and long tweed coat.

Over my dead body, Lauren thinks, but she smiles and nods politely as her father disappears.

———

A fresh gown has been deposited at the foot of her bed, but the nurse's aide who left it there has vanished. The next time an actual nurse materializes, Lauren asks for help in getting out of her old gown and into the new one.

"Oh, I don't *do* that sort of thing," the nurse says, as if she's been asked to give advice on where to go to procure the services of the hottest hookers in town. "Do it yourself, it's good for you," she orders. No smile of encouragement accompanies her behest; she's here to check Serra on the other side of the room, and the look she flashes in Lauren's direction strongly suggests that Lauren is nothing more than a particularly distasteful blood-sucking insect.

Bending from the waist, attempting to lean across the bed to grab the gown just out of reach, Lauren shuts her eyes against the pain. It just hurts too much; she'd rather lie here in her gown spotted with rust-colored blood from a leaky IV site than cause herself any further pain. This shames and worries her, as if she might be judged weak or lazy, but come *on*, wasn't it only yesterday that she had surgery? Isn't she entitled to a little help from these folks whose job it is to heal her?

B-I-T-C-H, she spells silently as the nurse leaves the room.

And for additional satisfaction, Lauren gives her the finger.

Shortly before dinner, an angel of mercy she hasn't seen before agrees to help. "I'll do whatever I can for you in the next three minutes," the nurse promises cheerfully. "But after those three minutes are up, my break starts. And you know I got to have my caffeine, right?"

In just under three minutes, Lauren gets a new, pristine gown patterned with fleurs-de-lis, though the sponge bath she's dying for has been put on hold indefinitely. This is one of Manhattan's finest hospitals, but here's one patient whose face hasn't been washed in over forty-eight hours and who is still waiting for a fucking toothbrush. She's a little bemused; how is it possible that she's been transformed into someone incapable of walking to the bathroom and washing her face on her own at the sink? Only two days ago, she had a pair of utterly dependable knees that could get her anywhere she wanted to go (even up the eighty-six flights of stairs to the top of the Empire State Building, if necessary). And, oh yeah, also a fiancé who presumably loved her enough to spend the rest of his life in her company.

She looks over at Serra, who, in the presence of her elderly mother, is devouring what appears to be a Big Mac or its Burger King equivalent. Lauren can smell that supersized order of fries from across the room. Her own mother is gone from this world, but, in any case, she probably couldn't have been persuaded to bring even the tastiest junk food to Lauren. She was done in by a spot of melanoma that spread, disastrously, to her brain, just after Lauren moved in with Alex. And she is still sorely missed two years later. Her mother's ideas about food, Lauren recalls, were a little wacky during her childhood: only five M&Ms, one of each color, were allowed every night after dinner. And only half a Twinkie, the other half wrapped and put away in the refrigerator, where it remained until the following night when Lauren was permitted to finish it.

If her mother had been luckier, she'd be fifty-eight years

old now, still a middle-aged person with, presumably, much to look forward to. And with, presumably, some good advice for Lauren—who could use a little hand-holding as she sits in her hospital bed eyeing the sweetness with which Serra's mother pushes Serra's hair from her face and arranges it behind ears so large and cupped that, well, only a mother could love them.

"Enough, Mommy, leave it, I just wanna eat my dinner, okay?" Serra says in annoyance.

Hearing this big, ungainly, chronically ill fifty-one-year-old refer to her mother as "Mommy" makes Lauren's heart hurt, as her own mother used to say.

Though Alex had apparently been fully prepared to send her packing, he hasn't once, in this first week during which Lauren has been homebound and glued to his bed, mentioned even a word about her departure. Beyond that, he's been so attentive, so utterly deferential, that if Lauren didn't know better, she might almost be convinced he's forgotten his particular grievances (still unnamed) and fallen back in love with her. Each morning before leaving for work, he prepares a tray to fit over her lap, arranging a small glass bowl of cat-shaped mini-cookies from Trader Joe's for her breakfast, and for her lunch, a Saran-Wrapped peanut butter sandwich, a navel orange, and a Granny Smith apple. All Lauren need do is reach for it at the foot of the bed, a feat of which she's now capable. There's a brand new mini-fridge at her bedside, stocked with bottled water and cans of Diet Coke. Several times throughout the day, Alex calls to check on her, and when he returns at night after first stopping at the grocery store (formerly *her* responsibility), he prepares dinner for them both (also *her* responsibility), which Lauren eats in bed and which he eats seated on the floor next to her bedside, his plate resting on his knees, a glass of wine nearby. Afterward, he goes off to do the dishes. And, twice this week, a load of laundry (half Lauren's responsibility). All of this uncomplainingly.

Maybe it's guilt that has made him ever more attentive. The hard truth is, she can't survive without him right now, and he knows it.

They both know that if he were to kick her to the curb, Lauren would have no choice—with that ankle-to-hip brace on her leg—but to move in with her father and his exasperating girlfriend, Roxanna. An option that would probably make killing herself an attractive alternative.

———

Of the numerous humiliating favors Lauren is forced to ask of Alex, one of the most humiliating of all must be requested every night at bedtime. Now that two weeks have passed, and the sutures have been removed from her knee, she's finally permitted to shower every night. But there's a catch.

"Alex!" she calls. She knows he's in the living room watching *Animal House* on HBO and doesn't want to be disturbed. Can't she at least allow him to enjoy his movie in peace? But she has already undressed (by no means a minor accomplishment) and is waiting, a trifle impatiently, at the side of the bed for Alex to wrap a thirty-dollar water-proof plastic bag around her leg. Because even though the sutures are gone, the brace itself still has to remain dry in the shower.

Sitting in her bikini-cut underwear and favorite black bra, she calls Alex's name one more time, trying not to appear too needy. Though of course she's never been needier in her life.

When he arrives, a couple of minutes later, he ignores Lauren as she takes off her bra and bikini panties (a miserably obvious sign right there that, two weeks after her accident, he's undeniably no longer interested in her—not in *that* way, at least) and goes straight for the water-proof bag he generously charged on his MasterCard at a store called Medi-Supply across town on the Upper East Side. Its taxicab-yellow plastic is uncomfortably chilly against Lauren's skin, but she keeps that information to herself, not wanting to sound like a complainer. She eases herself timidly, painfully, into the shower, and settles, with difficulty, onto a small plastic bench meant for handicapped people like *her.* Alex closes the shower door behind her and waits for her to dismiss him. Lauren wants him to stay and keep an eye on her, but hasn't she asked enough of him? *Thank you,* she mouths from behind the clear glass door of the shower, and then he's off to see the rest of *Animal House,* the movie conveniently frozen in place by the miraculous technology of their digital video recorder.

The hot water, as it streams across her body, offers Lauren a bit of sensual pleasure, though certainly nothing like sex with Alex used to. Sex with Alex; isn't that the sort of notable pleasure she will never again experience with him? After much prodding, just a few days ago she finally learned—over a homemade dinner of soy burgers adorned with brie and mushrooms, and made-from-scratch sweet potato fries—Alex's chief reason for wanting her to take a hike. "Okay, look, the thing is, we're just not soul mates," he announced from his seat, the tiniest sliver of sautéed mushroom clinging to his neatly groomed beard. "To reduce it to a very basic level, I like the Beatles and you pretend to like the Stones."

"What are you *talking* about?" Lauren said. "Of course I'm your soul mate. I love you!" she said indignantly.

He shook his head. "We definitely feel affection for each other, we enjoy each other's company, but, at the end of the day, we just don't have that soul mate vibe." What he meant, Alex explained, is that while he failed to see the virtues of opera, Broadway musicals, and Charles Dickens, Lauren had never been enamored of Indian food, science fiction, or David Mamet.

Well, maybe so. But what did any of this have to do with love?

Lauren hates the expression "at the end of the day." And, at that moment, she was pretty sure she hated *him.* "Oh, for God's sake," she said. "Do you really think I could love someone who wasn't my soul mate?" Only minutes before, using a metal walker, its legs tipped with rubber so she wouldn't slip, she'd made her

TODAY IS NOT YOUR DAY

way laboriously down the hallway to the dining room, where Alex helped her into her wheelchair; positioned at just the right angle, it allowed her to sit and eat at the table. Like an ordinary person, not some loser who had to take all her meals in bed. But if, as Alex said, she failed to hold her own in the soul mate department, well, didn't *that* render her a loser?

No matter how vehemently Lauren protested, Alex could not be persuaded. "You saintly social worker types are all the same," he went on. "Thinking that the rest of the world can never rise to the occasion. Well, you know what? I can't spend a lifetime with someone who doesn't fully embrace the person that I am, i.e., a guy who makes a damn good living out there in the business world."

His accusation, after the more than two years they'd spent together, might almost have been funny, Lauren thinks, if only it hadn't been so infuriatingly wrongheaded. Not to mention insulting. Because she's not some snob, not someone who thinks that the measure of a man or woman is necessarily to be found in what they happen to do for a living. The truest measure of a man is deep in his marrow, isn't it? And look what a good soul Alex has proved to be in all the time she's known him; he's the good-hearted guy who marches every year in the Making Strides Against Breast Cancer Walk in memory of his best friend's mother; he's the uncle who showers his two little nephews with extravagant electronic toys; he's the one person Lauren knows who never allows himself to get entangled in family arguments but will, instead, work as a peacemaker to keep his family intact.

It is this goodhearted peacemaker who so recently informed her—during that dinner of soy burgers and fries—that as soon as the brace was off her leg and she could get around reasonably well on her own, she would have to find herself someplace else to live. In the meantime, Alex has continued to be helpful and solicitous; really, Lauren couldn't ask for a better home health-care attendant. And this is how, brokenheartedly, she has come to think of him—as a live-in, impressively conscientious healthcare worker. Someone who will meet all her physical needs except one.

Lauren calls his name now; she's finished in the shower, and needs help stepping out and then onto the bathmat. She can dry herself off, but needs help, as well, getting into her underwear and flannel pajama bottoms. Holding onto the edge of the sink and obediently lifting one foot and then the other so that Alex can get her panties on her, she feels like an overgrown, ungainly child who has failed to keep pace with her peers.

"I'm sorry," she says. "I hate to bother you." In the aftermath of her hot shower, the edges of white wallpaper patterned with black-and-gray confetti curl up slightly around the mirror above the sink. This is the same wallpaper that she and Alex spent half a day putting up together when she first moved in with him; afterward, Lauren remembers, he slowly lowered the straps of her overalls and slipped her T-shirt and sports bra over her head, admiring the look of her, topless, reflected in the mirror, her hair drawn back in a small knot, her feet in black flip-flops imprinted with peach-colored sea shells. Making love with him on the bedroom carpet just beyond the bathroom, dressed only in her flip-flops, Lauren listened closely, taking delight in the urgent sound of Alex's breathing in her ear.

She stares now at the chipped, did-it-yourself silvery polish remaining on her toenails. No professional pedicures on that skimpy take-home pay of hers.

Forbidden to put any weight on her bad leg, she's beholden to Alex for the smallest, most commonplace things: every night he holds her firmly around the waist as she stands on one leg in front of the bathroom mirror and uses both hands to floss her teeth. Without him, she might lose her balance and go crashing to the ceramic-tiled floor.

"Close your eyes," Lauren instructs him now, because it's just too creepy to have Alex watch her floss. "I'm sorry," she repeats.

"Apologize again and I'll blow your fuckin' head off," he

says casually, repeating a line they both love from the TV show *Deadwood*. They laugh together for the first time in three very long weeks and it feels like something to savor.

———

At night, in bed, forced to sleep flat on her back or on her side instead of in the fetal position she's always favored, Lauren gazes at the cottage cheese ceiling overhead, aware of Alex's gentle snoring beside her. How strange it is to be sharing a bed with someone who no longer wants her there. Occasionally, in his sleep, Alex casts an arm around her and unknowingly pulls her close. She snuggles up to him as best she can, her bum leg rigid in its brace. It feels dishonest, somehow, as if she's taking advantage of affection unconsciously offered by this man who, during waking hours, has carefully explained why he wants her out of his bed, out of his apartment, out of his life.

She hasn't yet shared the news with her father or with any of her friends that the wedding is off. As long as she and Alex appear to be a couple, living, as they still do, in the same apartment, why bother to spill the beans? Her father and friends feel sorry enough for her as it is because of her stupid accident; garnering even more sympathy from them would just be too much.

———

Sometimes, on weekend afternoons, after he returns from biking, Alex takes her out for a spin in her wheelchair, and Lauren waves gaily to the doorman as she whooshes by.

Sometimes she's out on her own, using her walker on a wintry day, forcing herself to make it to the Starbucks on the corner, amazed by the white-haired old ladies in the neighborhood who, in comparison with Lauren and her halting baby steps, seem to move like the wind.

———

"I'm not going to hurt you," her physical therapist promises, but at first Lauren doesn't believe him. He is a thoughtful, middle-aged Polish guy from Krakow; his eyes are a stunning turquoise, his hair pitch-black and stick-straight. His name is Tomasz and Lauren finds herself wondering if his father, who was a teenager during World War II, threw rocks at his Jewish neighbors before they were rounded up, forced into the Krakow ghetto, and, soon enough, hustled off to the gas chamber. (If he could read her mind, would Tomasz ask her to leave his office and make her promise never to come back?)

He treats her with something approaching tenderness; he undoes the Velcro flaps of her brace and lifts her leg from it so gently, it's as if he's unwrapping some treasure, one of those $5 million Fabergé eggs speckled with 3,000 tiny diamonds, perhaps. Frowning, he assesses Lauren's thin, pale leg, pure-white skin peeling sickeningly, and says that when he's finished with her, several months from now, she will be able to bend her knee considerably more than the ninety degrees required to walk up and down even the shortest flight of stairs.

Sounds great, Lauren says. Since she's currently incapable of descending into the subway, taking cabs to work, which used to be a luxury, is now a necessity. And way too expensive for someone whose salary is really just peanuts.

She has excellent health benefits, though, and so is able to visit Tomasz three times a week. As usual, today she sits on an upholstered table in one of the offices Tomasz shares with two other physical therapists. She is dressed for the occasion in gray yoga pants and a Harvard B School T-shirt. Standing alongside her, Tomasz extends her leg and raises it until the sole of her bare foot is resting against his shoulder. He tells Lauren about his aging parents, who still live in Krakow and somehow managed to survive first the Nazis and then the Communists.

Over the past couple of weeks, she's found herself confiding in him the way, she imagines, other women confide in their hairdressers. (*She*—the ill-paid social worker—doesn't have a hairdresser per se; her hair can be trimmed every few months in any neighborhood salon by anybody at all for about twenty-five bucks, tip included, and she's absolutely content with that.) Today she and Tomasz return to the subject of Alex and how the two of them had met online and the swiftness with which he'd invited Lauren to move in with him.

"Ah, love at first sight?" Tomasz says, and lowers her leg to the table.

"Something like that," Lauren says ruefully. "But now it looks like we're over."

"You want me to 'friend' you on Facebook and make this boyfriend of yours jealous?" Tomasz offers.

"That's sweet of you," Lauren says, "but I don't think that's going to help any."

" 'Facebook helps you connect and share with the people in your life,' " Tomasz recites, sounding like a commercial. He's been in the US for seven years and is still hoping to improve his already excellent English, the nuances of which he's learned from watching television. He asks Lauren to roll over onto her stomach now, and attaches a four-pound weight to her bad leg. "You are a Jewess, yes?" he says. The tone of his voice is pleasant, conversational; he might just as easily be asking, "You are a vegan, yes?"

Lauren's face burns, but isn't it Tomasz who should be embarrassed? "I'm *what*?" she says. Because isn't it just possible she's misunderstood him?

"You know what they mean by an Ashkenazi Jew, yes? I read an article in the *National Geographic* that says these particular Jews have the highest IQs of any people in the world. They are the smartest and the most accomplished. And since I believe you are a Jewess—yes?—I thought it would be nice for you to hear this. And now I want you to lift your leg slowly, very slowly, ten times, with the weight on it like this. Then rest, and do another ten. I have to check on another patient and soon I will be back."

She's on the honor system here; when Tomasz returns

and asks Lauren if she's done her leg-lifts twenty times, she can lie and say that she has, and he'll never know the difference. The reason for lying, Lauren understands, is this: the slower her progress, the longer it will take before Alex deems her fully dump-able, ready to be kicked out of what she still deludedly thinks of as "their" apartment.

See, they don't call those Ashkenazi Jews smarty-pants for nothing.

———

Lauren's six-week, post-op check-up is not going well. Her surgeon, who is just about her age (Lauren Googled her and knows that her husband is a weekend anchor on MSNBC and quite a hunk), reveals that she is disappointed in Lauren. The doctor wears impressively high heels, and one of those tiny phones smartly in her ear, and she walks with the hint of a swagger. As is befitting for a very busy surgeon inhabiting the world of sports medicine.

Alex, looking every inch like Lauren's significant other, smashes his knuckles together and furrows his brow. "You promised us the brace would be off in six weeks," he says. He sounds plaintive.

"I warned you guys at the beginning—your physical therapist needs to *hurt* you, Lauren," Dr. Gilchrist says. "But I can tell by your not-great progress that he's a wuss."

Sitting upright on the examining table, Lauren swings her good leg and looks down at the floor. "Tomasz is a sweetie," she reports.

"Well, he sounds nice but not like someone who's going to whip you into shape so that you'll be back to commuting to work on the subway every day," Dr. Gilchrist says. "You and your PT guy need a wake-up call."

"So the brace isn't coming off?" Alex says. His hands are in the front pockets of his jeans now, and he's taken a step back from Lauren and the examining table.

"Not at the moment, no. And that's because your progress, Ms. Bachman, is worthy of a B, B minus, when you should, in fact, have been striving for an A plus."

Lauren's always been such a diligent student, but now, of course, she's a deliberate failure. And who knows how many more weeks with Alex that crappy grade may have earned her!

"Lemme show you something," Dr. Gilchrist says. She takes Lauren's bad knee and bends it for her, viciously, as Lauren yelps in pain. On a scale of one to ten, Dr. Gilchrist's manhandling rates a ten. "*That's* the kind of progress we're interested in," she says. She pats Lauren on the shoulder. "Try harder," she advises.

Lauren's heart is thumping mightily; her knee is killing her. She'd like to get Dr. Gilchrist on the table, take a hard-faced ball-peen hammer to *her* left knee and see how the doc likes it. If it's tough love Dr. Gilchrist is advocating, why not show her exactly what she's referring to? Lauren thinks.

During the cab ride home, she and Alex silently retreat to their separate corners in the vinyl back seat patched in several places with white adhesive tape. And then, while stuck in rush hour traffic on upper Broadway, Lauren watches as Alex's arm suddenly extends toward her and his left hand seizes her right. They haven't held hands in she can't remember how long—at the very least, six weeks—and she foolishly allows this small, familiar gesture to inspire the tiniest whiff of hope to take root in her big dumb heart.

The shower seat, along with the thirty-dollar plastic bag that was formerly necessary to waterproof her leg, are sitting in the foyer, soon to be offered up for adoption in the laundry room of Alex's building, where tenants and owners leave all manner of things for anyone who might be able to make use of them. In just a few minutes, Lauren will be headed for her father's apartment in Mount Vernon, where he and Roxanna will show her to her room, an alcove, really, right off the dining area, where she can camp out until something better comes her way.

Isn't there anything she can say to Alex that will do the trick? He continues to insist that the two of them aren't soul mates and never were, but Lauren swears, right here in the lobby of Alex's building—surrounded by a couple of her carelessly packed suitcases on wheels and three jumbo-sized shopping bags stuffed with books—that they are. She murmurs a few other things as well, keeping her voice down so that the doorman and concierge can't hear the sound of her last-ditch effort to reclaim the guy whom she knows, whom she swears, to be the love of her thoroughly well-intentioned but ultimately ordinary life. Right here in this vast lobby decorated with wine-colored leather couches and matching club chairs, big brassy pots of identical arrangements of slightly dusty silk flowers.

"I *know*," Alex says. He rubs his thumb absently against the dry heel of Lauren's hand before going out to hail the cab that will shoot her straight to her father's doorstep. Where Roxanna, his live-in girlfriend, teetering on the brand new, high-heeled suede boots he bought her, will greet Lauren with what appears to be genuine enthusiasm as her father looks on approvingly.

Sweetie! Roxanna will say, and the whistle of her sibilant "S" will make Lauren's heart sink even lower.

AFTERLIFE

⋮

THOMAS HIGHFIELD WAS THE NAME of the man who'd been sent by her publisher to photograph Sharon for the shot on the flap jacket of what would turn out to be her one and only book. And he'd said something then, twenty-six years ago, that she'd never forgotten. Posing her carefully in front of the tiny built-in bookcase in her foyer, behind the flight of stairs that led to a sleeping loft, he'd adjusted the cant of her head with a pair of small, delicate hands and murmured, "Don't kid yourself, honey, the camera does nothing *but* lie." Sharon had looked at him, startled, but he refused to offer her anything more, though he did, in fact, shoot what emerged as the very best photos of herself she'd ever seen. A week or so later, examining the thumbnail-sized pictures on the contact sheet with a magnifying glass, she and Peter, married since the end of college and still in their twenties at the time her book was to be published, marveled at the way Thomas Highfield had somehow managed to capture, again and again, the very best that her face had to offer—the sweet diffidence and modesty of her smile, the luster of what appeared to be her perfectly black, nearly shoulder-length hair, the sparkly light of sheer happiness reflected in her dark eyes. Thomas Highfield was an eminent photographer, an artist, surely, and he had photographed her at what would prove to be the most gratifying time of her life. She was then, in the early Eighties, a young wife and mother, and about to become a respected novelist as well, someone whose book would eventually sell enough copies to land her, briefly, on the lowest rungs of a couple of bestseller lists.

She is hard-pressed to fathom just why, exactly, she is thinking of all this now—and of Thomas Highfield in particular—as she stands before Peter's freshly dug grave, their daughter, Violet, at her side, Violet's arm wrapped solicitously around Sharon's shoulders, Violet herself sniffling loudly as Jordan, her boyfriend, offers her the full-sized box of pale green Kleenex he's so thoughtfully remembered to bring along to the cemetery.

Oh, Jordan—what would they do without him? He's kind of a big, untidy mess of a guy, Sharon thinks ungenerously, but also a warm presence who's been a loving partner to Vi these past few years, and a loving father to their daughter, Emma, whom Vi gave birth to a couple of years ago. Emma was brought into this world with the help of their "birth team"—a midwife friend of theirs and a doula who, Vi had explained to Sharon, was a professional labor companion hired "to facilitate an empowering birthing experience." (Hearing those words, which struck Sharon as some sort of psychobabble, she nevertheless found herself wishing that, twenty-seven years earlier, *she* had been treated to an empowering birthing experience of her own, instead of the emergency C-section that had been performed when her blood pressure fell so suddenly and precipitously.)

The rabbi on the scene at the funeral today, a woman in her early forties with her car keys clutched in her gloved hand, begins to pitch the keys from one palm to the other, singing a Hebrew prayer in a noticeably impressive soprano. Sharon listens, dry-eyed; it is Vi and—unexpectedly—Jordan who are sobbing out here on this raw January day one week before what would have been Peter's fifty-sixth birthday. Grief, Sharon has decided, should be a private affair. Someone once told her this, years ago, at a family funeral she attended, and though she can't remember who might have said it, she nods her head now in agreement, uncomfortable with the showiness of Vi's and Jordan's weeping, the sort of weeping which strikes her as a little sloppy and undignified. And sloppy and undignified can't even begin to describe the matching chartreuse Crocs worn by both Vi and Jordan, cotton socks visible, as well, in the gap between the elasticized hem of their sweatpants and the rim of their plasticky shoes. Honestly, what could they have been thinking when they'd dressed themselves this morning in the spare bed-room of Sharon's Manhattan apartment? That they were going to the gym? To the 99 Cent Xpress? To the supermarket? As she studies them in their funeral finery, it's difficult for Sharon to keep herself from thinking, *Where did I go wrong?* On the other hand…how superficial can a person be, judging one's daughter and her boyfriend by the clunky plastic shoes they'd chosen to slip on their feet before heading out by cab from the city to this densely populated Long Island cemetery ornamented with the thin, pure-white crust of yesterday's snow.

Rabbi Wagner is still playing with her car keys as she explains that though Jews are generally skeptical of the notion of an afterlife, the memory of Peter will surely live forever in the hearts of those who loved him best. "By love are they remem-bered and in memory do they live," she recites. Vi and Jordan sob even louder at this, and then Jordan approaches the casket, which is covered by a gray wool blanket decorated with a large Star of David outlined in royal blue. He begins to address the crowd of a few dozen mourners—mostly fellow teachers from the prep school where Sharon has taught English for over two decades since her writing career tanked and from the community college where Peter was a dean, and where, less than a week ago, he was found slumped over his desk, cruelly felled by a massive heart attack. He'd lingered four long days in the cardiac ICU before dying.

"Oh, and for those of you who may not know me," Jordan interrupts himself, "I'm Peter's daughter's partner, and someone who totally loved him." He holds tight to his box of Kleenex, pressing it against his bulky middle; scrutinizing him, and then Vi, Sharon finds herself wishing that Jordan and Vi were both thinner, better-dressed, and—to be completely honest—maybe just friends instead of partners. But this is who they are, and, along with two-year-old Emma, they've formed what Sharon recognizes to be a genuinely happy family.

But her mind wanders now from Jordan's honeyed eulogy, and Sharon has to struggle to stay sober as she imagines the eye-rolling she and Peter would have indulged in together at the sight of those ridiculously irreverent Crocs embellishing the cemetery today. Suddenly she is seized by a fit of giddiness so overwhelming that she has to turn her back on the eulogy, on the rabbi, her friends and Peter's, and even the casket yet awaiting its final destination. She walks off in her high heels—*your fuck me pumps*, Peter loved to call them—and doesn't answer when she hears, only a moment later, her daughter's voice calling after her. The impulse to snicker has faded, replaced now with a burning in her throat and chest. She is bereft, she realizes. Utterly.

There was once a time when fifty-five or fifty-six had seemed ancient to her and Peter, when it conjured images of both sets of their parents, all four of them retirees in sunglasses half-dozing on chaises-longues under that generally reliable Fort Lauderdale sun, images of fifty-somethings endlessly discussing the neighbor's grandchild who'd blackened his family's name by peeing in the shallow end of the condo's pool. But fifty-five was, once Sharon and Peter had reached it themselves, simply the middle of their lives. Because, after all, they who'd rocked to Led Zep and Creedence Clearwater, who'd smoked weed as casually as their parents lit up Marlboros, who'd dropped acid once or twice before straightening out and enrolling in grad school, and who had, during their four years of college, slept recklessly with way too many partners, would, even so, live to the ripe old age of, say, one hundred and ten.

Of course they would, wouldn't they?

———

Now that Peter is gone, it's only the cat who plays the piano, strolling confidently across the keys whenever the spirit moves her. Now, though, Rose, the green-eyed, shaded silver Persian named for Peter's grandmother, is lounging on her favorite piece of living-room furniture, her ankles crossed gracefully and resting on the arm of the caramel-colored Ultrasuede couch. If Peter were here, he might be playing *My Funny Valentine* from his Rodgers and Hart anthology or *Embraceable You* from his Ira Gershwin songbook, accompanying the piano with his own sweet, perfectly pitched baritone. He'd played well, and with pleasure, and both he and Sharon were disappointed when Vi couldn't be persuaded to keep up with her piano lessons after a single lackluster year fraught with one too many arguments over whether or not she'd actually practiced a full half hour on any given day.

Peter has been gone just seventy-two hours, and already Sharon misses the sight and sound of him at their baby grand. And will discover, soon enough, moment by moment, everything else suddenly absent from her days on this earth.

She's decided to dispense with the ritual of sitting *shiva*, she and Peter having been only the most secular of Jews, the kind who hadn't bothered to enroll Violet in Hebrew school because it interfered with her starring role in the gymnastics programs that consumed so much of her childhood and adolescence. (Until, one day, late in her high school career, when Vi hung up her leotard for good, tired of the endless, wearying practices and meets and the struggle to keep her weight down to the bare minimum;

in her case, a meager ninety-two pounds. Her muscles have, since then, turned to mush, though her legs are still slender, her hands and feet small and surprisingly narrow.) And since there's no *shiva*, there's just Vi and Jordan keeping Sharon company here in the living room the day after the funeral, Jordan leaning across the couch to stroke the cat's well-padded belly. Like Vi and Jordan, Rose the cat could no doubt benefit from a carefully fine-tuned diet and a lot more exercise, Sharon notes guiltily, thinking she and Peter should have bought her a trial membership in the feline gym in their Upper East Side neighborhood and also started her on Tender Vittles Lite (less fat, more fiber!). She herself has been thin for years now, not that this makes her a superior person, she knows, but perhaps one possessing an ounce more self-control.

"We should call Emma," Jordan says. Lifting a long flap of Violet's hair, he plants an awkward kiss on the underside of her neck. "I miss my little girl," he says. Emma has been left behind with Jordan's mother in Framingham, near Boston, a better place for her than this grieving household, everyone, including Sharon, had agreed.

"*Our* little girl, and don't you think I miss her, too?" Vi says; she and Jordan, dressed in their sweats and Crocs again, argue for a minute about who will get to make the phone call. Vi gives in, a little sullenly, and then Jordan is on the phone in the galley kitchen, opening and closing one cabinet after another as he talks, the telephone cord soon entangling itself around his knees, reminding Sharon of those chains that prison officials wrap around the most violent offenders. Disengaging himself from the curling plastic wire, Jordan says, "Oh, she *did*?" He rubs one hand back and forth across his Grand Canyon souvenir sweatshirt. He has a management position in a factory outside of Boston that manufactures private-label mascara, eye shadow, and other cosmetics; according to Vi, there are a couple of hundred people working under Jordan. This is impressive, Sharon supposes, but she wishes that her daughter had fallen for someone a soupçon more intellectual. Not that Vi, who works as an office manager for a small law firm in Cambridge, is much of an intellectual herself; she's never made it all the way through *Samurai Worriers*, that one and only novel of Sharon's. Vi has attempted to read the book several times over the years but has never made it past page forty or so, she's told Sharon apologetically and more than once. *Something about it just doesn't, you know*, speak *to me*, she explained, each time shrugging her shoulders a little dismissively. And each time Sharon's face burned with both mortification and a glimmer of anger. You'd think she would have gotten over it by now, this failure of her own flesh and blood to appreciate the one truly impressive thing Sharon's accomplished in her life. She and Peter had discussed it again and again, beginning all the way back in the Nineties, once Vi had reached adolescence and was, they thought, sophisticated enough to read the book that Sharon had invested with her heart and soul. At its center was a woman who discovered, upon her husband's death, that during the course of their long marriage he'd hidden a pitch-dark, secret life as an occasional cross-dresser and jewelry thief; though he'd had some close calls, in the end he'd gotten away with it. The idea for the novel sprang from an article she'd read in the metro section of the *New York Times* when Vi was an infant and Sharon a stay-at-home mother in the city, and it took her less than two years to finish, thanks to Coreen, a baby nanny so thoughtful she anointed Vi's cheeks with Vaseline whenever she took her outdoors those first few winters of her life. The week Sharon finished the book, she'd called her friend Brett, who was an assistant editor at a publishing house on Madison Avenue, and though Brett had been engrossed in watching *Masterpiece Theatre* on PBS when Sharon called (and seemed indifferent to Sharon's nervously delivered oral synopsis), she did phone back after the show was over and agree to read the novel. Hearing, ten days later, that the book would be published was, Sharon would always say—even decades later when it was clear she wasn't really a writer but only someone who happened to have written one very good novel—unquestionably the best moment of her life. Or at least the most thrilling.

"Yeah, no problem," Jordan is saying, apparently still talking to his mother in Framingham. Then his voice turns gleeful. "No way!" he says. "No fucking way!"

"Hey! I miss my baby, too, you know," Vi calls out, and signals to Jordan to bring her the phone.

Jordan is whispering now, turning the broad expanse of his back to Sharon and Vi, ignoring Vi's request for the telephone. From her seat on the couch, Sharon stares out the living-room window at the sliver of orange sky visible between a pair of high-rises in the distance. The truth is, she wishes she'd been able to give birth to another daughter after Vi—Vi whom she loves deeply, but with whom she has nothing in common. *Nothing.* This other daughter would have a doctorate in English lit, she's fantasized, and would have read Sharon's novel two or three times, savoring it all the more with each reading. Unlike Violet, she would occasionally have the urge to wear a dress or skirt here and there and would display excellent taste in shoes, preferring high heels for work and chic leather flats on weekends. If there's one thing Sharon knows for certain, it's that this imaginary daughter of hers wouldn't be caught dead in a pair of Crocs. And neither would the imaginary daughter's boyfriend/partner/lover/whatever.

Feeling guilty for having conjured up this lovely daughter—a young woman so urbane and stylish—Sharon takes one of Vi's hands and gives it a swift, dry kiss. She starts to tell Vi that she's contemplating a walk, maybe a quick visit to the supermarket around the corner for a couple of oranges and a package of raisin bread for tomorrow's breakfast. But Vi is out of her seat now, striding toward Jordan with a vehemence that strikes Sharon as mystifying, and even a bit frightening.

"Just give me the damn phone, please," Violet orders, and when Sharon calls out to her and Jordan in the kitchen, asking, lamely, if everything is okay, all her daughter says is "Shush!"

Delivered in a hiss, not a very nice way to speak to your newly widowed mother, Sharon thinks.

On her way out, she rides the elevator down to the building's recycling room, where she drops off a shopping bag stuffed with old newspapers, all of them dating back to the weeks before Peter's death, before the heart attack itself. A time when Sharon was innocent of even the most remote possibility of losing her husband, who'd recently had his yearly check-up with his internist, a man not much older than Vi who'd pronounced Peter in damn good shape for "a relatively young guy." And she and Peter had a good laugh over that, about being deemed "relatively young" when, in their own minds, *of course* they were still young! She smiles now, after dumping the shopping bag into a large canvas recycling bin, remembering how Peter used to nag her, though good-naturedly, to read and recycle the piles of *New York Times* that she allowed to accumulate in their den week after week. Peter himself read everything online and couldn't understand why Sharon insisted on what was for her the pleasure of spreading the paper out in her lap and turning the pages at her leisure, tearing out articles or sections of articles to be gathered in a folder and then photocopied for her students. *They're not infants*, Peter reminded her every week. *Just email them a link to the articles.* But this was her way and she wasn't going to listen to him.

Would never have the opportunity to listen to him ever again, she acknowledges now.

She nods politely at the woman waiting at the elevator with her, a woman about Sharon's age dressed in a silvery, ankle-skimming chinchilla coat. The woman, Sharon observes, is wearing scuffed, slightly soiled Nikes with her fancy fur, a fashion statement that reminds her of precisely what she has decided *not* to think about for the rest of the afternoon—that being Vi and Jordan. And the seed of what had blossomed into a distressing argument between those two, the essence of which Sharon couldn't quite get a handle on before escaping the apartment.

"I'll tell you," the woman says after she and Sharon arrange themselves in the elevator, "I had to go to the post office and then I had to go home and fight with my husband. And now I'm going back to the post office again."

Smiling vaguely, Sharon says nothing. She would like to point out to the woman just how fortunate, how blessed, really, she is to have a living, breathing husband she can go home to and argue with as fiercely as she pleases and to whom she can offer an apology or two whenever it suits her. Sharon would like to point out that, at this moment, she would consider giving— and this isn't hyperbole—her very *life* merely to hear the familiar sound of Peter's gentle complaining: *Just read it online like everyone else, babe!*

The woman is looking at her in the elevator now, scowling. "My brother keeps insisting his grandchild is a prodigy, but frankly, we've yet to see a single shred of evidence."

The elevator door opens into the lobby. "Well, have a nice day in any case," Sharon says, though she doesn't mean it, not really, and is embarrassed to hear those insipid words flowing from her own mouth.

Maybe it's grief that's made her dull and stupid.

———

Violet is in the den, fooling with the TV remote and weeping softly when Sharon returns with her raisin bread and a couple of pints of ice cream in flavors that sounded too enticing to ignore: who could resist Brown Sugar and Crème Brulée? Screw the 20% fat content, the 285 calories per modest-sized serving. Give her a break: she's in the earliest stages of widowhood and doesn't yet know what the hell has hit her. It's a miracle she got to the market and back again without getting lost; she's that disoriented, that bewildered. That uncomprehending.

"Daddy wouldn't be happy to see you crying over him like that," she tells Vi. "And for what possible reason would you be sitting there watching *Dora the Explorer*?"

"It's Emma's favorite show these days," Vi offers, as if this were a satisfactory explanation. Blowing her nose into a tissue from the same box Jordan brought to the funeral, Vi says, "And anyway, I wasn't crying about Daddy."

"Are you all right?" Sharon asks, instantly wishing she hadn't. Because whatever it is Violet is going to tell her, she doesn't want to hear it right now. She eases the remote from her daughter's hand and clicks off the television. "Tell me," she says. Isn't this what a good mother does—encourage her child to unburden herself even when *she* doesn't feel strong enough to summon up more than a teaspoon of sympathy for those tears?

Violet curls her bottom lip, flings herself like a drama queen face-down onto the convertible sofa bed where she and Jordan have been sleeping each night since their arrival the night before Peter died. "It's Clare Breeze," she says. "And I'm not an idiot—I knew it, knew it, *knew* it," she adds. She weeps into a small, raspberry-colored velour pillow, ruining its velvety surface with her tears, Sharon can't help noticing.

"*Who?*" Sharon says. She sits down at the foot of the bed. "Who's Clare Breeze?" she says irritably. It's early evening; she doesn't understand why the sofa bed hasn't been folded up, the blanket and linens put away in the closet, and why Violet and Jordan's pajamas are littering the mattress, along with yesterday's bra, black and frilly. She's playing absently with the bra straps, tying them together in a messy bow as Vi flips herself over onto her back and explains, "When Emma was born, don't you remember? Clare was part of the birth team, the doula?" Now *she's* the one who sounds irritable.

"Oh, right, the person who 'empowered' you," Sharon says, gesturing with air quotes so that Vi will understand how much she despises the word. "So what *about* her?"

Sitting up and clutching the velour pillow, then wrapping

her arms around it in a full-fledged embrace, Vi tells her, weep-
ily, that Clare Breeze and Jordan had once, *a hundred years ago*,
been a couple. "So they, like, seem to have fallen back into their
old habit," she says, and hangs her head. Tears spill into her lap,
darkening her pale-gray sweatpants with a couple of small, dis-
tinct spatters.

"Seem to?" Sharon says. "I'm so sorry, sweetie. So Jordan
told you this just now, while I was out buying ice cream?"

"Of course not! You think I'm a moron? That I couldn't
figure things out for myself?" Violet sobs. "I'm not, you know,
an idiot. He was texting her in the kitchen, and I went in there
just in time to see those stupid emoticons—a string of little red
hearts. And some other squishy crap."

"O...kay...and where's Jordan?"

"Out," Violet snaps.

"Is he coming back for dinner?"

"How the hell do *I* know?"

Sharon sighs. If Peter were here, he would, she's certain,
advise her to stay out of it. In general, he was more at ease
than she with the notion of Vi-and-Jordan and their indiffer-
ence toward marriage, despite the fact that they'd had a child
together. (Unlike Sharon, Peter had never had a problem introducing Jordan as Vi's partner; for Sharon, it was different, a
clumsy phrase that never did slip freely from her small, rather
thin-lipped mouth.) She'd evolved—or maybe devolved—into a
fairly conventional person, Sharon had to admit, despite having
come of age not long after the freewheelin' Sixties. *Oh, don't be
such a square, Grandma!* she can hear Peter teasing.

What would he think if he knew that only three days after
his death, she's already surfed the Web, hunting for ways to find
him? *There are a variety of routes you may follow to see, hear, and
feel the energy of someone who has died*, one of the websites assured
her, and who is Sharon to question the claims of those who are
far more spiritual than she'll ever be?

"Please don't cry," she urges Violet, nearly a quarter of a

century ago a tiny five-year-old, smaller and more endearing than every one of her classmates at the touchy-feely private school she attended, little Violet a lovesick kindergartner who, during school hours, missed her mother so much that it made both their stomachs hurt. Nearly every afternoon Vi had been sent to the nurse's office, where she was permitted to call home and encouraged to let Sharon know just how much she longed for her. And every afternoon of that especially difficult school year, Sharon would say, "Well, thanks for sharing, baby," and then hang up on Vi, returning to the IBM Selectric typewriter on the desk in the large walk-in closet that served as her home office, still believing that she herself was a writer, a novelist, someone with more than one story to tell. This belief would turn out to be a serious miscalculation on her part, of course, but who knew, back then, that she was so off the mark, that the disappointment she would soon come to feel would not let up for years, like chronic back pain or early-morning stiffness in a bad knee. And maybe she'd been a bad mother, hanging up every day like that on five-year-old Violet—who might have thought, though she never said so, not then or at any other time, that Sharon hadn't loved her quite enough.

"I love you, baby," Sharon reassures her now, but Vi lets it go without even a shrug, and is back on the subject of Clare Breeze, whom Sharon envisions, from the sound of her name, as a tall, serene beauty with the perfect posture of a dancer.

She stretches her arm across the sofa bed to pat Vi's knee, and is shocked at the swiftness with which Vi draws both legs up to her chin, as if stung by her mother's innocent touch.

"You don't *know*," Vi insists. "You don't."

Well, maybe not, but doesn't she see how hurt Violet is? Sharon's not going to point out to her that she herself has just suffered a loss unequal to any other in this life of hers, and that she cannot imagine feeling any worse than she does at this very moment. She murmurs Peter's name, and hearing it, knows that her grief and Violet's are of two distinctly different qualities.

And feels all the more diminished because of it, feels an ache of loneliness so profound, so fierce, really, that she lets out a small, wounded cry that could be mistaken for the sound of someone in physical pain.

"We had a baby together!" Vi is saying, outraged. "And he's the one who went online looking for a doula for me and reconnected with this Clare Breeze and brought her into my hospital room, where, I have to say"—and here Violet's voice softens—"she was really pretty great, massaging my stomach with these nice scented oils, playing this New Agey music she'd downloaded onto her iPhone for me. While Jordan, the big loser, was freaking out and basically useless."

The sexy black bra is in Violet's hands now, and she stabs her French-tipped index finger *(that one surprising concession to femininity,* Sharon thinks) straight through a piece of sheer lace, pushing her finger through twice and then twice more, expanding the hole until, finally, she can put her small, angry fist through it. And then casts the bra disgustedly to the floor. "Jordan ordered this stupid bra from Bloomingdale's online, seventy-two dollars, I saw the credit card bill," Violet says. "He gave it to me for Valentine's Day last year, but do you think I care?"

Sharon shakes her head dutifully in response to this question that requires none.

"Damn straight I don't care. All I care about is that those two are hooking up again, like they were back in high school. Crazy, right? I mean, what the hell is he *thinking?*" The look on Violet's face, as she stares in Sharon's direction now, is anguished. And immediately Sharon tries to summon up Jordan's best qualities—his warmth, the tenderness with which he shelters little Emma in his big, spacious lap, the joyous way he carries her around hoisted on his extra-wide shoulders—so that she, Sharon, can truly understand the depth of Violet's misery.

But her heart's not in it; not now, when her own pain is full strength and there are no measures she can take to dilute it. She can't see her way past it, can't see how she can possibly offer

Violet the consolation she's looking for. Maybe another time, but not today, not now.

Instead, taking in the sight of her grown daughter lying around weeping on an unmade bed just after sunset, all Sharon can think—uncharitably, she knows—is *Get over it, kiddo. And while you're at it, can you please get your act together and read my damn book?* Because here's that other thing she can't let go of: even after all these years (more than a decade since Vi's been old enough to read *Samurai Worriers*), Sharon is still deeply insulted, still pissed off by her daughter's failure to get beyond page forty, her failure to give her a little credit for the one thing Sharon wants, more than anything, to be remembered for.

She allows herself to recall, here and now, that long and wonderful afternoon she hung out with Thomas Highfield, a man who'd photographed Richard Nixon, and also Sharon's heroes John Updike, Susan Sontag, and Saul Bellow. That afternoon, though, there was only Sharon herself—a quietly optimistic twenty-something striking one unassuming, slightly self-conscious pose after another for Thomas Highfield in those three or four hours they spent in each other's company. Until finally he must have known that they'd got it just right, Sharon's young face perfectly radiant, the sheen of her bright future soon to be reflected back at her from the thick, glossy paper of her book cover. The camera faking it, as usual, telling one more big fat lie to anyone at all who cared to take even a moment's notice.

M.I.A.

ACCORDING TO MY SHRINK, Dr. Wintergreen, the disappointments I'd had with women could all be traced to a single fact: that, as a child, I'd rarely had the opportunity to burrow into the warm nest of my mother's lap. Dr. Wintergreen had a shaved head that gleamed in the soft light of his office, and he bit his nails ferociously during my forty-five-minute appointments with him. From the start, I found it humiliating to unravel my life before a perfect stranger, and after a handful of sessions, I decided to walk away. It wasn't until much later—until after I'd married Molly and moved to Stamford and until my seven-year-old stepson, Jack, and I had fallen into the habit of lounging on the couch in the den together every night—that I gave any real thought to what Dr. Wintergreen had said about my mother. Jack would ease himself under my arm and lay his head in my lap; the two of us would watch reruns of *The Simpsons* and *Modern Family*, and I found myself wondering every so often if Jack's life as an adult would be any happier for it. He was a sweet-faced first-grader who usually called me Will (but sometimes, weirdly, "Uncle Dad") and had a father of his own living in a neighboring town.

I'd hit my thirty-fourth birthday shortly before Molly asked me to marry her. She never actually pronounced the words, but coyly presented me with a flimsy, nearly see-through white T-shirt that read: "Will You Marry Me?" in white felt letters that she'd sewn on by hand. More than a little startled, since we'd been together barely six months, I told her I needed a minute to catch my breath. (Only later did I realize that, at the very least, I probably should have planted my mouth against hers for even the briefest kiss.) Molly said it was totally fine; she understood that I might want a day or so to think things over. "No worries," she said. "Take your time."

Though no one ever wore it, the T-shirt somehow ended up in the laundry hamper in the master bathroom, where it remained buried forever beneath layers of pajamas and socks and underwear that, unlike the T-shirt, eventually saw the light of day again.

Molly was someone who knew how to seize control of a situation. When Richie, her first husband, announced he'd fallen out of love with her, she hauled off and punched him, hard enough to fracture the bridge of his nose. (On the way to the ER, with her pissed-off husband beside her, she drove so fast that she was pulled over by a cop and given a $200 speeding ticket and points on her license.) The two of us met on OkCupid several months after Molly and Richie separated, which wasn't much longer than a week after their frenetic trip to the ER. Those first emails of hers were peppered with smiley face emoticons and an excess of exclamation points, which normally would have turned me off—permanently—but for some reason I was intrigued nonetheless. Maybe it was because she included *Anna Karenina* and *Abbey Road* as, respectively, her favorite novel and Beatles album. The black-and-white photo of herself she inserted into an email showed someone in her early thirties with a lively face and long wavy hair brushed neatly over one shoulder. I hadn't been in love in what felt like a painfully long while, and was pretty much convinced I was one of those people who would never get what I wanted most in this world. What I actually wanted was a family—a wife and multiple children; even an in-law or two thrown into the mix was fine with me. I was an only child. My mother died when I was three and a half, and I was raised by a woman from Trinidad named Nell, someone I felt more deeply connected to than my own father, a sociologist who remarried when I was in high school. My father and his new wife decamped to Claremont, California, the summer after my graduation. This was around the same time that Nell's daughter and grandchildren moved to Atlanta, and Nell had chosen to go along with them. She sweetly and lovingly checked in with me from time to time, never failing to mention the framed photograph of my four-year-old self that hung on her new living-room wall along with those of her grandchildren. In Claremont, I discovered on my first trip out there, my father had no such photograph in his living room, den, or anywhere else. He was, I understood, devoted to his new wife and his teaching job at Pomona. These were facts that could not be disputed.

During the time between college and my marriage, I'd earned a master's degree in public health and found a job with a non-profit in Manhattan. And I'd been in love with three different women, each relationship lasting a couple of years. But each time, I saw that marriage would have been a serious misstep. The women I fell for tended to be too much like me in their failings—moody and indecisive and all too easily disheartened. Molly, however, claimed that there wasn't enough time in the day for her to be depressed; she was just too busy with her job and her child. She seemed to possess an enormous amount of energy and couldn't understand what I thought was so wonderful about sleeping until noon every weekend. The second time I stayed over at her house, she had me out of bed and reading the Sunday *Times* by nine. By ten, all of us were swimming in the indoor pool at the Y, Jack happily attached to my shoulders, looking, I bet, as if he unmistakably belonged to me. That morning, I taught him how to dive off the side of the pool. We worked at it for well over an hour, and when Jack finally caught on, we celebrated with shouts and high-fives so raucous the lifeguard blew his whistle at us in annoyance.

Less than twenty-four hours after Molly's proposal, I accepted. There hadn't been a lot for me to think about, really. I was in love with her and could readily imagine our life together. She was strong-willed and clearly thought well of herself (though not in a way that gave off even a flicker of arrogance, I observed), and I realized that I was drawn to her because of those very qualities that I myself often seemed to lack. On a mild, midsummer afternoon a few months later, we were married in Molly's back yard, with a couple of bridesmaids in short black dresses and bare legs, groomsmen in an assortment of pale suits, and Jack as the ring boy. I wore an immaculate white suit and Molly a flouncey champagne-colored dress and high heels with long steel stems like daggers. *Just like a real wedding*, I heard a geriatric guest say in a stage whisper as Molly and I made our way toward her brother, a newly anointed Universal Life Minister—certified the night before on the Internet—who was waiting for us under an 80-foot maple tree that stood alone at the end of the lawn.

Just like a real wedding. What the fuck is that *supposed to mean?* I wanted to ask Molly's elderly aunt, but I tried my best to forget it.

Not long before Molly and I met, she'd put in for a sabbatical from her job as an assistant principal at the local middle school, explaining to me that she'd worked too hard for too long and just wanted to savor the pleasures of being a housewife for a while. She turned out to be an exemplary one—closely resembling the kind on sitcoms half a century ago, one of those women who baked brownies from scratch and drove around in a station wagon crammed with a pack of noisy kids, one large but well-behaved dog, and brown paper bags of groceries ornamented with celery stalks that peeked out over the top. When I was a kid, I fantasized that my mother had been that kind of woman. She'd been gravely ill almost from the time I was born, and so I had, even during my childhood, only the vaguest memories of her—of a woman lying in a room so dark she could barely be seen. She couldn't possibly have been baking brownies or anything else, but that was the way I'd wanted to think of her.

At first my life with Molly and Jack was nothing less than completely gratifying, and so neatly structured that it made me smile to myself in pleasure on the train ride home from Grand Central every night. Dinner was always at 7:15, half an hour after I got home from work. Afterward I spent time with Jack and read to him before bed, and then Molly and I would catch up on our day and listen to music together before retreating to our separate laptops in the den. Once or twice a month we took Jack to the city for concerts at Lincoln Center and visits to the Guggenheim and MoMA, because of course it was important for him to be exposed to all the right stuff.

And I felt, at last, that I was living the life I was meant for—all that had come before it seemed hardly worth remembering.

Even after Molly and I have been married for several months, she's still referring to Richie as "the Creep." "The Creep and his little friend will be here in an hour to pick up Jack," she reports one Sunday morning in the fall. Richie's "little friend" is a med student in Manhattan and I sense that Molly is a bit in awe of her, although of course she will never admit it. I wish she would call Richie and Allyson by their real names; that she refuses can only mean she continues to view Richie's new life with bitterness.

I *get* it—I understand that eight years of marriage aren't

easily forgotten, but I know I won't be able to relax until I'm certain this part of Molly's life is officially, irrevocably over. In recent weeks it seems that she's been fighting with Richie at every turn, mostly over Jack-related issues—criticizing the gifts Richie buys him (a tiny gecko named Vinny that has to be fed crickets every day at mealtime, and a pair of smelly turtles with flowers painted on their shells), the places he takes Jack to eat (Arby's, Wendy's, Smokey Joe's BBQ), the hours he wants to see him (as close to 48 of them as possible every weekend). One time I make the mistake of saying, "Why can't you just give the guy a break?" and Molly tells me to mind my own business. I suspect that, in a way, it *is* my business, but I decide to stay out of it in order to keep things from getting messier than they already are. Jack is precious to me; the surprising, warm weight of the little guy's sleepy white-blond head against my neck as I carry him upstairs to bed is something I can't bear to think of losing.

The three of us are still at the kitchen table eating breakfast when Richie arrives one Saturday morning and immediately plunks down an aluminum foil-wrapped box in front of Jack. Though Richie and I usually shake hands, this time, feeling lazy, I just wave from my seat at the table as he stretches out his arm in my direction.

"We made orange French toast from a recipe in the *Times*," I say. "Wanna try a piece?"

"Richie hates French toast," Molly says, and then, to Richie, "So where's your little doctor friend today? I thought you two were inseparable."

Richie hesitates a moment. "Oh, she figured she'd better stay home and get busy on some big OB-GYN thing that's coming up."

"OB-GYN *thing*?" Molly says, sounding annoyed. "*What* thing?"

"I don't know, some exam she has to take."

"Don't call it a 'thing,' Richie. Don't be so vague."

Jack has torn the tin foil from his gift and is reading out

loud from the print on the box. "Rep-tangles," he says, and points to the colorful turtle-shaped pieces that, Richie explains, will help to teach him geometry when he snaps them together.

"Like a seven-year-old needs to learn about geometry," Molly says. "Come *on*."

"Thank you, Daddy," Jack says. He starts to empty the plastic pieces from the box, but stops obediently when Molly says, "Forget that and finish your breakfast, baby boy."

Richie walks over to kiss the top of his son's head, and I stiffen in my seat. When Richie isn't around, how easy it is to pretend that Jack's my own son, that what is between us can't be duplicated. But whenever I see Jack and Richie together, I'm reminded of the unequivocal truth, that the kid is loved by his father and returns that love easily.

"So where would you like to go today, pal?" Richie says.

"Bumper cars, please. I wanna go where they have bumper cars."

"Absolutely not," Molly says. There's a seeded bread stick in her hand and she snaps it viciously in two.

"Why?" Richie and I say in unison.

"How about because bumper cars are stupid and dangerous, that's why."

"Oh, please, you're being ridiculous," Richie says.

"He's right," I agree.

Molly rolls her eyes. "Really? Since when are you two on the same team? Honestly!"

Knowing what I have to do, I excuse myself from the table and, with the *Times* under my arm, trudge upstairs to the master bedroom. I take off the moccasins I use for slippers and lie on my side along the bed. I start to read an article about pollution in L.A. but can't concentrate because of the commotion that's going on downstairs. I hear Molly yelling; a door slams and everything is quiet. The door slams a second time and I know I'm alone in the house. Richie's house, the one he bought with all that money he earned from the big companies he designs websites for. It's insane—the house I come home to every night, the bed Molly and I make love in, the silverware I raise to my lips, all of it belonged to Richie not long ago. I've been dying, from the day I moved in, to convince Molly to sell the house, but she refuses to even contemplate the subject. She keeps saying she loves the house itself (just an ordinary colonial with an apartment in the basement for our nonexistent live-in help) and everything in it, and if I could only make the effort, I'd find myself feeling the same way. How she can possibly expect me to adjust to this bed the two of us share, I don't know—after eight years the mattress is thinned-out and droopy, and above it hangs a canopy ornamented with a quartet of fluted white drapes that belong on some depraved plantation in antebellum Louisiana.

More than once I've dreamt that I organized a garage sale where I got rid of everything; each time, the fucking canopy was the first thing to go.

Something that continues to surprise me is that I'm sort of fond of Richie, another thought I'll keep to myself. My guess is that if Richie weren't Molly's ex, the two of us might have been friends. It isn't that hard to imagine myself seated at some sushi bar with him in the city, listening sympathetically to the story of how Richie got his nose broken. I'm glad he has no idea how much I envy him, mostly for having found Molly and married her under the best of circumstances—uncomplicated ones. He and Molly had a child together and chose a home for themselves. Things fell to ruins, but that's strictly between the two of them and no one else. If marriages had to fail, they should all end like that—with nothing more complicated than a simple failure of love.

I've just fired up my laptop and switched to reading the newspaper online when I hear a noise at the bedroom window. I get up and see that it's Molly, pitching pebbles in the backyard to get my attention. I shove the window open and lean across the sill.

"How about we go to the movies?" Molly shouts up at me.

It's barely eleven o'clock, and a pleasantly sunny day. "You're kidding," I say.

"What do you mean?"

"I mean I can't go to the movies when the sun's out. There's just something kind of unseemly about it," I say in a loud voice.

"Come down and we'll discuss it."

"You come up. I'm still in my bathrobe."

"Get dressed, lazy boy."

I nod, and shut the window. I'm annoyed at myself for giving in to her, and I deliberately take my time getting dressed. I put on a plaid flannel shirt and my oldest, softest jeans. They date back to someone I was with before Molly—a very small, very quiet girl named Charlotte. Molly knows next to nothing about her—except that Charlotte and I went shopping for those Levis together—but she keeps trying to get me to toss the jeans, insisting they're a size too small and make me look like I need to start doing sit-ups every day. No one except Molly has ever accused me, even jokingly, of having a belly, and I'm insulted each time she brings it up. I stand now in front of the full-length mirror attached to the back of the bedroom door and study the jeans from every angle. Then I pull them off and stuff them into the wicker wastepaper basket next to my dresser; I can't believe how Molly has tainted my pleasure in them.

I'm sprawled on the bed Googling stores that sell mattresses when Molly comes upstairs. "So what's taking so long?" she says mildly. She sits cross-legged on the floor and looks up at me. She's smiling at me now, but I don't know what to make of it. I don't ask what she and Richie were fighting about or whether Jack is going to get to those bumper cars today after all. Maybe it *is* none of my business. The thought makes me lonely, almost lonely enough to call my father in California. The two of us haven't spoken in over a month, though we text from time to time, usually about TV shows my father likes to recommend— *Sherlock* and *Downton Abbey* on PBS, and documentaries about the Japanese and the Germans and their atrocious behavior in

World War II. My father is not a fun-loving guy. Or much of a father. He didn't even bother to come to our wedding, choosing instead to attend a conference in Honolulu on examining the intersection of race, class, and gender. (Though at least he sent a gift, a check for $5000, which Molly was impressed by. And though we needed the money, I would have preferred that he ditch the conference and show up at the wedding instead. I've imagined complaining about his absence to Dr. Wintergreen, imagined my former shrink nodding sympathetically, as I can remember him doing—though only occasionally.)

Molly is still smiling.

"What are *you* so happy about?" I say.

"I don't know, maybe I'm just relieved that the Creep's gone for another week."

"Can you do me a favor, please?" I say. "Can you please not call him that?"

"Didn't know it made any difference to you one way or the other, sweetie."

"It gets to me," I say.

"I can't help it. You have no idea what it was like for me. There I was, thinking I was a happily married person, and then out of nowhere came this piece of news I couldn't make any sense of. For weeks after he left, the only thing I could eat was yogurt—everything else made me want to puke." Molly pauses, wraps a dark hank of hair across her eyes like a blindfold. "I was a champion sleeper in those days. Jack and I went to bed at the same time, if you can believe that. Eight o'clock and the day was over for me. Even so, it wasn't nearly enough sleep, believe me."

Why is she telling me this stuff I don't want to hear? "All right," I say. "Enough. Forget it." She was married for eight years and that's all I need to know—the rest she can keep to herself. I don't want to hear about how much she used to love Richie or anyone else. It's better to waste a sunny afternoon inside an empty movie theatre, locking hands with her in the dark until one of us feels a cramp setting in and has to let go.

I happen to find myself on the phone with Richie one night when Molly is out late shopping at the mall in Stamford. It's the longest conversation he and I have ever had with each another.

"So what's up? What can I do for you?" I ask, trying not to sound too friendly. I've got a DVD on; I'm watching Robert Redford fighting for his life on the open sea and wish I hadn't answered the phone.

"For starters, dude, you can tell your wife to stop leaving messages for me at my girlfriend's apartment. Allyson's not running an answering service, okay? Why can't Molly just call me on my cell? Or text me."

"Are you drunk?" I watch as Robert Redford carefully shaves his 77-year-old, still-handsome face, and then I say, "Did you and Allyson have a fight over this?"

"We had what I'd like to call a discussion, and after that I had a good part of a six-pack to fortify myself and after *that* I called you."

"Well, Molly's not home."

"That's fine," Richie says. "Because you're the one I wanted to talk to anyway."

"Hmm, I don't think so."

"You're the only adult in that house who's got his head screwed on properly, dude. Your wife's got things all confused."

"Well, I'll be sure to tell her you called," I say, though I know even at this moment that I won't.

"Are you hanging up now, Will?"

"Frankly, I'd really like to."

"Hey, why don't you come over here and help me finish off this six-pack?"

"Sorry, I'm babysitting."

Richie lets out a sigh, followed by an exceptionally loud burp. "I hope you're not pissed at me for telling you stuff you don't really wanna know. Are you pissed? Be honest, okay?"

"No worries," I say, and I'm about to hang up when Richie tells me to hold on.

"Wait, did you guys ever find Vinny?" he asks. Vinny, Jack's new gecko, a three-inch little velvety-green guy with a few crimson spots here and there, has been missing since last weekend.

"Nope, he's still M.I.A.," I report. "And Jack's pretty upset."

"I'll get him another one, no problem."

"The problem is, he wants *Vinny*."

"Well, if Vinny doesn't turn up, maybe we can take Jack shopping for a ferret or something."

"Cool," I say. I don't really mean it.

I go to the medicine cabinet in the powder room off the kitchen and swallow down some Advil with a lukewarm sip of water, even though my head hasn't started to hurt yet. According to a pharmacist friend of mine, anything you take for a headache needs to be in your system for a full forty minutes before it does any good at all.

The next time Richie comes to pick up Jack for the weekend, I make sure I'm away from the house. It's another of those near-perfect fall days, the air clear as can be; carrying a waxy white bakery bag full of stale bread to feed to the ducks, I walk a couple of miles to the small, man-made pond Jack and I like to visit together. A mallard with a green head and a white-ringed neck approaches, squawking bitterly, and, without warning or apology, steps on my foot. I offer it a small piece from a rock-hard baguette, and it's quickly snapped from my fingers. The mallard follows me to the edge of the pond and jumps in clumsily, splashing puddles at my feet. There are dozens just like this guy in the water, and a handful of swans, elegant-necked, serenely making their way from one side of the pond to the other and back. I toss a piece of baguette into the pond; several ducks go for it at the same time, colliding with one another so hard that feathers fly.

"Take it easy, boys," I murmur, and pitch them most of what's left in the bakery bag.

Across the water, members of a wedding party are arranging themselves to be photographed on an ornamental bridge that arches over part of the concrete path circling the pond. The photographer accompanying them is running up and down the bridge, trying to get everyone in order. I walk slowly in their direction, flinging bread into the pond as I saunter by. I stop at a stone bench close to the bridge and sit down. I smile at the bride, but she's studying the sky with a worried expression. Looking up, I see that the sky has gone from bright blue to the palest gray, and the sun has disappeared.

"Shit shit shit," the photographer grunts. He stamps his foot. It begins to rain lightly, and I watch as the wedding party flees to the limos parked in a neat row of four on the grass beyond the concrete path. I know the marriage will never last; I can already see the wedding album full of the bride's anxious face. *Look*, I imagine her saying, slowly turning the pages of the album for her brand new significant other. *It's clear in almost every picture that it wasn't going to work.*

The rain is falling hard now; I take off for home, running along a commercial street, past some drugstores, a bowling alley, a library. Then I turn off into a residential neighborhood and slow down. I'm out of breath and there are streaks of pain beneath my ribs. I take it slow the rest of the way home. When I get there, Richie's ancient MG in its original British Racing Green is parked in the driveway; I'm annoyed by the sight of it. I enter the house through the side door and walk to the end of the kitchen. Keeping both feet on the ceramic tile that's meant to look like slate, I gaze past the dining room to where Molly and Jack—and Richie—are playing Monopoly on the floor. Molly is whispering something into Richie's ear, her bare arm draped over his shoulder; Richie is smiling faintly. Jack is seated between his father's legs. There's a pair of dice cupped in his small palm and he's twisting his wrist back and forth. Though it's only the second week in

November, a fire is burning in the brick fireplace and there are three mugs, three spoons, and three napkins on a teakwood tray near Richie's feet.

"Hey guys," I say, but so softly that no one hears. "What's up?" I call out, and the three of them turn their heads toward me now. "Hey, it's just me, your lawfully wedded husband," I say to Molly, and give her a small smile that matches Richie's.

"Oh my god, do you know what you look like?" Molly says.

"A drowned rat?" I stand in the doorway of the kitchen, shivering. I'm afraid to move farther into the house; I don't want to drip all over the expensive carpeting.

I sneeze twice.

"You should have some hot chocolate," Jack says, and very carefully carries over one of the mugs from the tray.

"Why don't you get him some towels," Richie tells Molly. "And a bathrobe or something." He gives her a gentle push in my direction. "What are you waiting for?"

I sneeze again as Molly picks herself up and goes to the linen closet.

Richie says, "So Jack wanted to stay home and play Monopoly, and I couldn't talk him out of it."

"Don't say it like that, Daddy," Jack says. "You *love* Monopoly even though you sound like you don't." He touches my hand. "Are you too sick to play with us, Uncle Dad?"

"Me? First thing I'm doing is getting myself into a hot shower, buddy."

"Here you go," Molly says, returning with two towels, a big one that she wraps around my shoulders and a small hand towel that she uses to wipe my face, as if I were a young child or a very old man.

In fact, I am neither.

I shed my Nikes and socks and go upstairs. Once I'm out of the shower and in my goofy, extravagantly large terrycloth bathrobe, I walk down the hallway to the bedroom and close the door behind me. I can't decide what to do; it's as if I'm fifteen,

back in my father's house, trapped in my room while he enter-
tains one of his girlfriends downstairs before the two of them go
out to dinner. My father had any number of girlfriends—at one
time, I remember, there were two women he was seeing during
the week and a third he saw on weekends only. But he was always
reticent about the women he was dating; it was as if he were trying to shield me from some terrible truth. The truth was, I didn't
care in the least about my father's social life, but I kept to my
room because I sensed that made it easier for both of us. Just as
I'm making it easier for Molly. Because only a blind man could
have missed the way those three looked, seated so cozily around
the Monopoly board; only someone completely clueless could
have missed Molly waiting there in her living room, watchful for
Richie's change of heart.

Molly is asleep under the canopy when I emerge from the
bathroom tonight, swiping an errant spot of toothpaste from the
bottom of my chin. The room is dark except for the reading lamp
on my side of the bed. I'm about to turn it off when I happen to
glance beyond me at the industrial gray carpeting flecked with
bits of color and see what looks like a tiny plastic lizard that Jack
has carelessly left behind. But when I reach down from the bed
to pick it up and place it on the night table, the green plastic
thing springs to life, turning its head slowly and deliberately to
the left to stare at me. This is no plastic lizard, and this, I will
swear, is the most terrifying moment of my life; underneath my
pajamas, gooseflesh rises instantly along the length of my arms
and legs. No one has ever looked at me this way, so coldly and
so clearly; I try to awaken Molly to let her know. I put my hand
on her arm and squeeze. "Molly!" I say. And then I say her name
again, this time more urgently.

"Not now, baby," she murmurs. "Not now."

GREAT JONES STREET

WHAT SHE LOST, exactly, was nine months of her life. This was fifteen years before the end of the twentieth century, when Mel was still a teenager and worried parents everywhere were still years away from being able to hunt down their kids on cell phones.

It began with those bean-shaped swollen glands in her neck that failed to shrink back to their normal size; the chemo and radiation that followed left Mel weakened and bewildered, and bald as her ancient great-grandfather (who was so old, he'd been born, astonishingly, at the tail end of the nineteenth century). Even her eyebrows and lashes vanished. When she was feeling up to looking into a mirror at her startlingly smooth head, she had a few brief, agonizing thoughts of death, but really what she feared most was that forever after she'd look like a freak, some androgynous creature from a distant galaxy. Many months later, when her hair had grown in all the way to her chin, glossy and thicker than it had ever been, she couldn't keep her hands away from it, as if it were something beloved that might be stolen from her at any moment.

Her body took its own sweet time repairing itself, and while her friends went off to their junior year of high school, Mel studied chemistry, trigonometry, American history, English, and French—all with a home tutor named Evan Chase, a spectacularly good-looking guy in his late twenties who showed up four times a week and sat at her bedside on a throne-like dining-room chair, his long legs stretched casually in her direction. He seemed to regard her as just another student temporarily laid up in bed with, say, an ankle that had been fractured in three places on the slopes somewhere in Vermont. This pleased her no end, and after a while Mel began to imagine that she was in love with him.

At the start and finish of each tutoring session the two of them talked of things other than schoolwork, and eventually she learned that Evan Chase sometimes worked as a fashion model, mostly for catalogues and posters for department stores. A couple of times he'd booked jobs with the Gap and Banana Republic, which, he told her—though only after she'd pressed him—she could check out in old issues of *Esquire* and *Vanity Fair*. His wife, Celine, was a model, too, and when he pulled out a snapshot from his wallet (those were the days when people still carried pictures in their wallets), Mel admired it politely, agreeing that of course Celine was beautiful. In her daydreams, Mel killed off this stranger in a dozen plane crashes that took Celine's life instantly and painlessly. She pictured herself healthy and strong and with a full head of hair that Evan gently trailed his fingers through just before his lips reached hers. As the two of them went over polynomials and conjugated irregular French verbs, she wanted to seize his hand and tell him what was really on her mind. Once, Evan brought her a gift, a baseball cap from a Mets game he'd gone to with Celine; while he arranged the hat sideways on her head, Mel told herself that under no circumstance would she take it off, that if she were actually dying, she would leave instructions with her parents to bury it along with her in her coffin.

When, at last, it was clear that she was well enough to return to school, just in time for final exams, it hit her that she would not, in all likelihood, see Evan Chase ever again; it wasn't, after all, as if the two of them were real friends, people who might see a movie together or go out for Chinese food on a Friday night. He had sweetened a miserable time in her life with his companionship, buoyed her spirits immeasurably, only to be transformed, suddenly and cruelly, into a figure from her past, a memory she could conjure up effortlessly if she wanted to. Walking the steamy, un-air-conditioned hallways of the high school that June, impersonating an ordinary teenager in a base-ball cap, she mourned Evan and the fantasies that had nourished her like nothing else in all the months she'd been absent from the world.

The closest of her friends, crazily, improbably, all named Lisa (Miller, Goldman, and Ornati—sounding like a law firm), had called and visited her whenever they could during those nine months. There was plenty of room for Mel in their lives again once she was well, and she found herself absorbed back into their little group, lying idle all summer long around the pool at the local swim club, hoping the cutest cabana boys would take notice of them and their blossoming figures. It was only then, stretched out in the sun for hours at a time on a vinyl chaise longue, that Mel allowed herself to fully acknowledge that her illness might have killed her, that the terror she'd glimpsed in her parents' middle-aged faces, the faint muffled sound of her mother's sobbing late at night, wouldn't be forgotten anytime soon by the three of them. And it became clear that her mother and father had lost faith in their comfortable suburban lives, now touched with pain every time they thought of how they might have lost her, might lose her still, despite the oncologist's assurances to the contrary. (After all, Mel had heard her parents whisper over the phone to their friends, he was only a doctor; he wasn't *God himself*, for crying out loud.)

Her mother, in particular, seemed impossibly slow to

recover, suddenly turning weepy as she emptied bags of groceries onto the shelves in the pantry or channel-surfed the TV, searching for something she could distract herself with for half an hour. She'd always been breezy and sociable, with a wide circle of devoted friends with whom she played mah jongg and drove to Manhattan to the theatre for Wednesday matinees. Passionately (maybe even obsessively so, Mel sometimes thought) interested in her appearance, Nina had a closet full of trendy clothing and shoes, much of it so ill-chosen that, in Mel's embarrassed eyes, her mother occasionally looked like an overgrown teenager in her vivid pink or turquoise high-topped Reeboks and the sweat suits that matched them. But when Mel had fallen so seriously ill, her mother had withdrawn from her friends and taken to dressing, day after day, in the same black leggings and almost comically baggy T-shirts. She no longer bothered with lipstick and eyeliner, and let her frosted blonde hair grow out into a lusterless brown filigreed with silvery-gray. And she devolved into the sort of mother who—once Mel was in remission—waited like a watch dog at the front door for her return from the movies or an occasional rock concert or party, and then greeted her with an extravagant, theatrical embrace, as if Mel had just emerged from a car that was about to explode in flames. Her mother tried, without much success, to keep her on a short leash, allowing her out at night only after the two of them had fought with each other for so long and at such a pitch that her father had to intervene. A reticent guy who normally preferred to keep to himself even within the confines of his own family, he almost always took Mel's side, begging, "Give her a break, Nina," in a voice etched with resentment and sometimes, it seemed, bitterness.

"Why is it," her mother is saying one night that summer, her fingers clamped in a tight-fitting bracelet around Mel's slender wrist, "that I'm the only one in this family smart enough to realize that you can't just go running off with your friends all the time as if nothing's happened, as if you haven't been through something so horrific that—"

"That *what*?" Mel says irritably; her mother is just too annoying. The three Lisas are out in front of the house; she can hear the rude, insistent bleating of the Toyota's horn and imagines the Lisas leaping out of the car and marching up the lawn, yanking open the screen door and boldly pulling her from her mother's grasp.

"That we still need to keep close watch over you every—"

"Every minute of the day?" Mel shrieks. "Every day for the rest of my life?"

Reluctantly, it's clear, her mother lets go of Mel's wrist. "These fears of mine happen to be perfectly normal ones," she says. "You and your crazy father think otherwise, but I guarantee you that ninety-nine point nine percent of parents who've lived through the horror that I have—excuse me, I mean that *we* have—absolutely see things the same way."

Appearing in the living room now, just a moment or two after Mel has lost her composure, her father concedes, "Yeah, maybe." He's slouching against the keyboard side of the piano, embracing himself, eyes narrowed at his wife. "But you'd better get your act together pronto, Nina, because frankly, I can't take too much more of this."

"This?" Nina says. "What's *this*?"

"This," Walter explains, "is all the screaming going on around here, all these battles of the wills...So ask yourself this, Nina: is this a place yours truly looks forward to coming home to every night? What do *you* think?"

"You selfish prick," Nina says, and as Mel looks on in astonishment—because surely this isn't the sort of family she's grown up in—her mother slaps her father across the face with the back of her manicured hand. Outside, the Toyota's horn sounds three long, exasperated blasts, and, without a word, Mel heads for the front door. Suddenly changing direction, she approaches her father and touches the small crescent-shaped puncture wound in his cheek, left behind by her mother's engagement ring.

"I'm sorry," Mel says. Her mother's flown from the room; it's just Mel and her father now, the two of them, as always, shy and vaguely uncomfortable in each other's presence. This strikes her, all at once, as something profoundly sad; unexpectedly, her eyes burn.

Her father nods. "If you think any of this is your fault, Mel, you're mistaken," he says. "Do you understand what I'm telling you?"

"Okay," she hears herself say. "I mean, no problem."

Her father appears relieved; his posture improves, and the pouches that hang beneath his eyes look slightly less mournful. "Good," he says. "Because I don't want any of this coming back to haunt us years from now."

"Haunt us?" she says, not quite certain what he has in mind. "Like ghosts?"

Reaching into the front pocket of his chinos, her father comes up with a ten-dollar bill and a small collection of quarters and dimes, all of which he hands over to her. "Take your friends out for pizza or something," he says wearily; tucked inside the crumpled bill are two slightly nicked Bayer aspirin, which Mel deposits in a flowerpot on the windowsill on her way out.

In the rear of the Toyota, seated next to Lisa Goldman, Mel lets out an impressive scream and drums her fists into her knees. "Sorry!" she says, as her friends stare, waiting for an explanation.

"Your parents giving you grief again?" Lisa Ornati says, and crunches the gears as she shifts into first. At the stop sign at the corner, slipping into neutral, she lights a cigarette, takes a deep drag, and passes it into the back seat to Lisa Goldman, who, Mel knows, wants more than anything for Lisa Ornati to stop regarding her as geeky. And maybe even earn her admiration. But Mel knows, as well, how much pleasure it gives Lisa Ornati to gently mock Lisa Goldman at every opportunity.

Of the three Lisas, it's Lisa Ornati who's Mel's favorite;

seemingly a little stony-hearted and judgmental, she wept when Mel told her that she was officially in remission and fit to return to school.

"My parents," Mel is saying, "are a real piece of work." She's about to say several things she knows are disloyal in the extreme, and decides instead to change the subject. "Hey, listen, guys, there's someplace I really wanna go," she announces.

"Hope it's somewhere cool," Lisa Miller says, up front beside Lisa Ornati in what all of them casually refer to as *the death seat*. "Because we're all bored out of our fucking minds."

What she means, Mel knows, is that there isn't a single decent movie left to see in all of Westchester, the malls are closed, and they can't get into any bars without fake IDs, which, to their disappointment, not one of them has been able to score.

Taking her second and final drag on the shared cigarette, Lisa Miller flicks it out the window in disgust.

"I have an idea," offers Lisa Goldman. "Why don't we go to my house and dye our hair with Kool-Aid? I've got some lemon-lime, which turns your hair kind of chartreuse, and also raspberry, which comes out a really nice pink. My sister did just her bangs the other night and she looks awesome."

At this, everyone listening snorts with laughter; Lisa Miller, always eager to play Lisa Ornati's lieutenant, says, "God, your sister's such a loser! How come you haven't figured that out yet?"

"Let's just go into the city, okay?" Mel says, her voice rising above Lisa Goldman's perfunctory defense of her sister. "Gas and tolls are on me."

Stopped at a red light now, the car idles noisily. It's seven years old and kind of a beater; its radio and air-conditioner have long been on the blink, but it's the only car Mel and the trio of Lisas ever have at their disposal, and all of them are grateful that it generally gets them where they want to go.

"Okay, but the city is huge," Lisa Ornati points out. "So what are we talking here—east side, west side, SoHo, TriBeCa, uptown, downtown, what?"

"Great Jones Street," Mel says. "It's between the Village and the East Village, I think." It's where Evan Chase lives with his eye-catching, dark-haired wife; the street name alone is enough to set Mel's pulse racing. She's tried not to fantasize about him too often, but now and then, as she coasts toward sleep after midnight, she indulges herself just a little, dispensing with Evan's wife, Celine, on an American Airlines flight to nowhere while Evan himself waits on Great Jones Street for the call about the plane crash that will send him directly into Mel's utterly sympathetic arms. She's confided to her friends only that she has a crush on him, though the phrase *hopelessly in love* seems closer to the truth and far more poignant, she thinks. The 8 by 10 headshot of himself—which he gave her the day of their final tutoring session—has his name printed in all caps at the bottom, and is hidden away in her dresser; kissing his full-lipped, unsmiling mouth just before she settles into bed at night is an unfortunate habit she's going to have to break, she's told herself ruefully. Sometimes she traces the perfect arch of his eyebrows (were they shaped in a salon? she wonders, and hopes not) and pretends to tousle his hair, leaving a smudge of fingerprints over the only photograph of him she has. She doesn't want to believe that she'll stay in love with him for the rest of her life, but hasn't yet figured out how to loosen the hold he has on her imagination. Maybe, she speculates, seeing him sauntering hand in hand with his wife on Great Jones Street will be enough to knock some sense into her stupid head.

"My sister used to have a boyfriend who lived in the East Village," Lisa Goldman is saying. "He was a percussionist in a jazz band and he only took a shower, like, once every two weeks. He stunk so bad. And his band stunk too."

"We *told* you she's a loser," Lisa Miller says, and pokes Lisa Ornati in the ribs.

"Not *that* sister. My other sister," Lisa Goldman says.

"Jesus, what a family."

"Can you please just forget about them?" Mel says. "It's Evan Chase we're gonna look for. Remember my tutor? I just feel like seeing him one more time."

"The model?" Lisa Ornati says. "Awesome."

"We'll never find him," Lisa Goldman predicts gloomily. "What do you think, he's sitting out on the front stoop just waiting for Mel to come by and make a fool of herself?"

But Mel's not going to make a fool of herself. "If we can't find him, at least we can check out where he lives," she says.

"Well, I'm game," Lisa Miller says. "We could use a little adventure in our pathetic boring lives, don't you think?"

Inside the Toyota speeding along the Bronx River Parkway with all four windows rolled down, Mel savors the feel and sight of her hair flying, like her friends', in the summer-warm breeze; not everyone, she knows, can claim to be so lucky.

They find their way downtown after a long series of blunders, and eventually cross the Bowery, arriving at last at Great Jones Street. The street, whose name had sounded so promising, so exotic and full of life, is dark and nearly deserted, lined with commercial parking garages and industrial-looking buildings. The whole street, in fact, appears ugly and sinister, a place where a woman hurrying by all alone might expect nothing but trouble.

"This is where Loverboy lives?" Lisa Ornati says. "You gotta be kidding." She keeps the motor running and fires up another cigarette, apparently waiting for Mel to admit she's had enough, that it's time to head back home to the suburbs or at least someplace safe and familiar.

"Well, he's got a huge loft up there," Mel says, leaning out the window of the car and pointing, "with a greenhouse, I think he told me. It's amazing, living in a loft," she continues, though she has no idea what she's talking about, and, in truth, has never set foot inside a loft, either in New York City or anyplace else. "It takes imagination to live in a big open space like that," she says grandly.

She forces herself to venture out of the car, and discovers

Evan's name just outside the entrance to the apartment building in a directory that lists three other tenants. There are numbers to punch, like a push-button phone, and she realizes that each tenant has his own personal, secret code, which of course Evan had never given her. And why would he? There's no connection between the two of them now except in Mel's imagination, a confused, forlorn place where airplanes crash silently at her bidding and an exceptionally attractive married man falls willingly into her embrace whenever she summons him. She's almost seventeen, old enough to give up a phantom lover with whom she has no future, she tells herself now. Sinking down onto the pavement in front of the building, she watches an enormous roach pass by with a fly hitching a ride on its back. Her stomach clenches; she shuts her eyes.

When Lisa Ornati comes out of the car to get her moments later, a fresh cigarette glowing between her fingers, Mel has her head resting across her raised knees, and can barely bring herself to look up at her friend.

"Listen," Lisa says, squatting down beside her, "you can't stay here. *We* can't stay here."

"I know. This has to be one of the nastiest blocks in the city," Mel acknowledges.

"So now you know where the guy lives," Lisa says. "Now what?"

"He kissed me once," Mel says. "The last time I saw him, he said, 'Take care now,' and kind of brushed his lips across my forehead." Sighing, she finishes, "I guess that's that, huh?"

"A kiss on the forehead, how fucking romantic," Lisa says, and rolls her eyes.

"Yeah, right."

"Get over it," Lisa advises. And then, softening, she pats Mel's shoulder. "Don't worry, we'll find someone else for you to lust after."

"You think it's so easy getting over someone who looks the way he does, like a celebrity, kind of? He was on *One Life to Live* for a few months. One day he's on the soaps and the next he's explaining the constitutional amendments to me."

"Bummer."

"Maybe for him, but not for me," Mel says, and she's smiling. "I couldn't take my eyes off him at first, I couldn't believe he was actually sitting in *my* bedroom, of all places."

A shirtless man in shorts and unlaced basketball sneakers shoots them a dirty look. "I hope you're swimming in a lake of fire—you and your whole goddamn freakin' family!" he calls out as he passes by.

Behind Mel and Lisa, on the other side of the building's glass door, a man and a woman appear in the vestibule; making their way outside, laughing companionably, they stroll toward the lights of Lafayette Street half a block in the distance, taking no notice of the two girls sitting on the pavement while they saunter past. Evan Chase is in jeans and red snakeskin boots; the small blonde his arm is coiled around is wearing perfume that smells like cotton candy, a scent that hangs offensively in the stagnant summer air as the two of them stop for a quick smooch. The woman sporting skin-tight jeans and stiletto heels is plainly not that darkly beautiful wife of his, and this small, vital piece of information hits Mel with the surprising intensity of a powerful blow delivered head-on. It kills her to think that, quite possibly, Evan is the sort of husband who doesn't deserve the lovely woman in the snapshot—the woman whom Mel has knocked off so casually in countless daydreams and whom she now feels strangely protective of. She doesn't, at age sixteen, want to believe that, in addition to the possibility of death rearing its ugly, gruesome head into her particular corner of the world, there's now *this* to contend with—the certainty that this guy swanning along Great Jones Street in his snakeskin boots is someone whose beauty goes no farther than those elegant cheekbones of his.

"You selfish prick," Mel murmurs, borrowing her mother's words, which have remained with her all night like a fierce headache that will not dim.

"What are you mumbling about?" Lisa says. "Was that him?"

"No way! Are you kidding—that was just some guy walking down the street in his stupid cowboy boots on a Saturday night."

"Well, *that* sucks," Lisa says consolingly.

Heading back to Westchester, Mel sits up front, playing with her wonderful new head of hair, hiding her face in its thick dark curtain gratefully. And then the bleak memory of another trip back home from the city sneaks up on her: there she was, she and her parents, caught on the parkway in a fierce snowstorm after a chemo session at Sloan-Kettering. Don't ask: while the blizzard raged beyond her father's Volvo, she lay in the back seat, rousing herself every so often to puke her guts out into the flimsy plastic bag from ShopRite her mother held open for her. Right there on the leather seat of the brand new Volvo, while her father cursed the slippery road and snow-flecked windshield and her mother fretted and ground her teeth, Mel had decided to pack it in, convinced that if this was life, she wanted no part of it.

"You get the picture, don't you?" she whispers to the three Lisas now, hopeful that, at this very moment, they're capable of a modest miracle or two and can read her mind—years before they will reach adulthood and lay claim to those unforeseeable lives waiting for them like lovers with a tenderhearted, welcoming embrace.

MANICURE

:
.

I WAS FIFTY-TWO, an underpaid teacher and the author of a handful of slender but critically acclaimed volumes of experimental stuff which I knew for a fact had been read by at least three people. Those were: my mother, my deceased father, and Sherri, my ex-wife, who, several years earlier, untied the knot that had legally bound us together for almost a quarter of a century.

Returning home after a deeply unsatisfying workout at the gym at the neighborhood Y, I was met in the hallway outside my apartment by the second-grader who lived a few doors down.

"How's it going, Gabriel?" I said. "Hard day at the office?"

Gabriel delicately scratched first one ear lobe and then the other. "Is your wife home?"

"Regrettably, she no longer lives here. And hasn't for a number of years. You know I don't have a wife, Gabe."

"Wull," Gabriel said. He had a high, broad forehead framed by a head of enviably thick, dirty-blond hair; he regarded me gravely.

"*Wull* what, Gabe?"

"Do you want a manicure? Kate, our nanny, said we could give you one." Pointing down the hallway to his younger sister, whom I could see was sitting on the floor holding a tray of some sort in her lap, Gabriel said, "Me and Nicole wanna make some money to buy a kidden. We only charge five dollars for a manicure, so do you want one?"

"What kind of *kidden*? Or kitten, as the case may be. And where's Kate? Why isn't she watching you?"

"A black one with a white face and long whiskers, okay? And Kate's making our dinner."

I put the key in the door, then turned to show my hands to Gabriel. My short, squarish nails were clean, perfectly trimmed, and unexceptional in every way, except for my thumbnails, which, unaccountably, were ridged like seashells. "You really think I need a manicure? I'll tell you what, Gabe, I'll leave it to your professional judgment, how's that?"

"Wull, Nicole has like a million different colors of nail polish and you could even pick a different color for each finger."

"Okay then!" I said, motioning for Nicole to join us. "Come on in, guys. But we have to be quiet because the baby might be sleeping."

Vanessa, the teenaged babysitter doing her physics homework on my living room couch, nodded. "I got her down about an hour ago," she reported. Vanessa was an experienced, good-humored employee wearing a T-shirt that announced, "I May Not Always Be Right But I'm Never Wrong."

"How come you have a baby if you don't have a wife?" Gabriel asked me.

"The baby's my granddaughter," I explained. "Though *her* parents aren't married either. They're on vacation and the baby is staying with me for a while. But listen, let's tiptoe, shall we. And let me take that tray from your sister." I escorted the two kids to the glass-topped coffee table, paid Vanessa and sent her home, which was only two floors down. Peeking into the master bedroom, I observed Whitney-Rose in her portable crib, sleeping with her little padded rump in the air, her lips pulsing. I wasn't much for babies, but this was a different case entirely—this was my granddaughter, after all, and I had to admit that I found her irresistible, despite the sheer dopey carelessness that had led to her birth. I especially admired her miniature hands and feet, which were, to me, anyway, infinitely kissable. And I now fought back the urge to drop a kiss or two on those very hands and feet; waking her, I knew, was ill-advised. Particularly since her "fussy time"—around five o'clock every day—was quickly approaching. This was the time when she turned mysteriously inconsolable, when holding her, rocking her, laying her down, rubbing her back, giving her a bottle, all proved worthless. Each day for the past three days, at approximately five o'clock, her worldview seemed to mirror that of my long-widowed, octogenarian mother, wherein just about everything was wrong and almost nothing was right. Unlike her great-grandmother, however, Whitney-Rose had already shown noticeable signs of abundant personal charm, smiling goofily when the spirit moved her and clinging tightly to my shoulder like a little chimp as I ferried her from room to room pointing out things of interest. Just before heading back into the living room now, I bent over and, what the hell, planted a soundless kiss just above her ear.

Nicole the manicurist was dressed in pink corduroy overalls and was waiting for me with almost a dozen bottles of Glimmer Gloss polish lined up neatly on her tray. I selected Grape Shimmer for my pinkies, Banana Blaze for my index fingers, Strawberry Sizzle for the thumbs, and Kiss Me Coral for the rest. But first, Nicole informed me, she needed to use her enemy board to file down my nails.

"Hmm, I think not. Take a look for yourself, Nicole. And that's 'emery' board, by the way."

"Nuh-uh," said Nicole. "*Enemy.*"

"Fine." I wasn't going to argue with a five-year-old, was I?

Nicole filed away industriously for a moment or two, then went for the Kiss Me Coral and my left hand, while Gabriel worked swiftly on the right. "It's like a coloring book," he told his sister wisely. "You gotta stay in the lines."

"Excellent advice that seems to have gone unheeded," I said, noting that my cuticles had been painted as well.

"You owe us ten dollars," Gabriel said as they finished up. "I get five and so does Nicole."

"The terms of the agreement say otherwise, Gabe. Five dollars is what you asked for and five dollars is what you get, okay? Lemme find my wallet," I said, and blew on my nails.

"Cheap bastard," Gabriel said, as casually as could be. He smiled winningly in my direction.

"That's naughty! We don't talk that way around here, for your information. And no wages until you apologize."

"What's 'wages'?"

"That's the money you get paid for doing a good job." I took another look at my multi-colored cuticles. "Or barely adequate, as the case may be." All I had in my wallet was a twenty, a ten, and three singles. "Say you're sorry you called me a cheap bastard and this ten is yours," I instructed Gabe, not a hint of enthusiasm in my voice.

"I'm sorry I said 'cheap bastard,' okay?"

"A pleasure doing business with you," I said, and handed over the ten. "And now it's time for you two to go on home and have your dinner." I watched as Gabriel held the bill in hand and scrutinized it intently. "That's Alexander Hamilton," I reported. "Great American statesman and secretary of the treasury, I believe."

"Okay, wait," Gabriel said, thrusting a small finger in the air. "If Nicole says 'cheap bastard' and then says she's sorry, does she get ten dollars too?"

I had to laugh. "What do *you* think?"

"Wull, I think N-O, but…"

"But nothing. N-O is right."

"I hafta go home," Nicole said, suddenly tearful, "but I don't know how to get there."

"Sure you do, honey, you're right down the hall," I said, but Nicole insisted she was lost and began to sob.

The doorbell rang three times; if the baby woke up, I resolved, whoever was out there on the other side of the door was going to get slugged. "Lemme answer that and then I'll take you home," I told Nicole, who was weeping impassionedly now, open-mouthed, her innocent, unspoiled little baby teeth a perfect, dazzling white.

"Hi there!" said Sherri, my ex. She kissed my cheek and looked me up and down. "Love your nails," she said. "I take it this is the new you?" She was in a red turtleneck, black leather pants, and ankle-high boots with fashionably pointed toes. Her formerly salt-and-pepper hair had been dyed the deepest black and appeared especially lustrous, I noticed. She'd been a chicly attractive woman when I married her long ago and was still a looker. Smart and self-confident, she was currently a high-end real estate broker and married to a urologist who specialized in kidney transplants. The truth was, I still loved her and had just about forgiven her for dumping me. (Though ultimately, she'd been the one who moved out, allowing me to stay put in our pre-war, high-ceilinged apartment on the Upper West Side.) This was the woman who, several years back, when asked what she wanted for our 24th wedding anniversary, had answered, simply, "A divorce." Not that I ever fully blamed her, not really. Because except for a couple of good years, decades ago—when I was awarded a handful of fellowships one right after the other—I'd been, throughout our long marriage, forever struggling to earn a decent living. And so I got it, at least partly, when finally Sherri lost patience with me. Like most people, she'd longed for certain things—a spacious, beautifully appointed home, a car that actually started when you turned the key in the ignition, vacations to Europe, dinners in good restaurants, clothing that wasn't bought on sale at 50% off—and I understood all of this. I would have liked some of those things as well, particularly a high performance car with a powerful engine—a Porsche 911, to be precise. But I continued to live without them easily enough, without much regret. I was a writer, and there was no escaping my calling. This, however, was old news. Since making a vow, several months ago, never to write another word ever again, it was a different ball game entirely.

"Who's that cutie over there who's crying so hard?" Sherri asked as she stepped into the living room.

"Oh, that's just Nicole, my manicurist. I'm about to accompany her home."

"My sister's a stupid crybaby," Gabriel offered.

" 'Stupid' is an ugly word," Sherri said. "And even more so when one is referring to one's little sister."

'What's 'one'?'

" 'One' means Y-O-U," I explained. I took Nicole gently by the hand and ushered her to the door. "Coming?" I asked Gabe.

When I returned, my ex had microwaved herself a mug of instant coffee and was chillin' on the love seat with her pointy-toed boots off. "I went and took a peek at our gorgeous little Whitney-Rose. Is she beautiful or what?"

"Make yourself at home, why doncha," I said to Sherri, and parked myself beside her. "And yes, she's a beauty all right." I reached over, grabbed my ex by the ankle, and lightly tickled the bottom of her foot. "You're looking pretty terrific, kiddo."

"Wish I could say the same for you," Sherri said, giggly as a delighted child. Reclaiming her foot, she elbowed me in the ribs. "I hate being tickled," she said. "As you well know."

"So you think I look like hell, is that it?"

"Kinda."

"Well, when I went to visit my mother yesterday, she raised her skirt and showed me her left thigh, right there in her living room," I began, "and I'm still recovering from the incident. She had some sort of rash, that's all. She just wanted my advice—you know, whether I thought she needed to see a dermatologist or a plain old internist."

Unsurprisingly, Sherri didn't want to hear about it. "Don't," she said, putting her index finger to my lips. "Do *not* share this with me."

"I was looking for a bit of sympathy, but evidently none will be forthcoming," I whined.

"Oh, I've got plenty of sympathy," Sherri assured me, "but one of the great pleasures of no longer being hitched to you is that I no longer have your mother to contend with."

"You lucky duck, you. And what are some of the other pleasures?"

"Can't think of 'em right now."

I smiled, and settled my arm cozily along her shoulders. "I keep thinking you still love me."

"Hmm," said Sherri. She paused. "So what's new around here these days?"

"Nothin' much. What's up with you and Jeff? How's the kidney transplant business? He still raking in the big bucks?"

Snuggling against me, Sherri said, "He saves lives, you know. Every day of the week."

"Yeah, but he charges an arm and a leg, doesn't he?"

"Very nice, funny boy."

I entertained myself picturing Jeff in a small, tight bathing suit; I could just see the guy's flabby upper arms, his chubby knees, and, most satisfying of all, the pot belly that spilled shamefully from the top of his neon-yellow Speedo. Not that I'd run into Jeff more than once—and in a meeting that lasted no longer than a fleeting, awkward moment or two. Alone and in line at the movies one night a couple of months after Sherri's wedding, I caught sight of her and her hubby emerging from the theatre, arm in arm, Sherri in mink earmuffs and matching jacket, Jeff on his iPhone, probably taking an emergency call from a panicked intern. Sherri and I had chatted while Jeff continued to talk into his phone. When he hung up, he and I shook hands courteously. I'd taken note of Jeff's neatly blow-dried gray hair and his cashmere overcoat. His shoes, no doubt Italian-made loafers, were a touch too soft and delicate-looking, I thought. And of course there I was, as usual, in my jeans and green-and-white suede Pumas and an old army jacket. I'd never in my life owned a cashmere anything, nor had I ever held a blow-dryer in my hands except to heat up a wet sock or two after a walk home from the subway on a rainy day. I'd guessed that Jeff took cabs everywhere and hadn't set foot on any sort of public transportation whatsoever in decades. In short, Sherri had chosen for herself a man who was my antithesis in nearly every conceivable way—a wealthy, blow-dried guy who probably didn't have a creative bone in his body, and who regarded me with utter bemusement.

"Sucks," I said mournfully now in my living room.

Sherri lifted her head from my shoulder. "What?"

"Oh, nothin'."

"Tell me."

"Forget it," I insisted.

"In that case," Sherri said, "do you think Whitney-Rose is going to wake up anytime soon? I need a baby fix—I need to hold her in my arms and give those chubby cheeks a big fat smooch."

"Rule number one in this home is that we never wake a sleeping baby."

"Well, I'm meeting Jeff for an early dinner at the Yale Club in about an hour and then we're going to the theatre, so let's hope she wakes up soon."

"Let's," I said, trying not to sound too despondent. "You done with this coffee?" I got to my feet and reached for the mug, its rim smeared with fresh lipstick.

"No, I'm *not* finished. You trying to get rid of me?" Sherri said.

"According to my well-kept records, you're the one who worked so hard to get rid of *me*," I said, and rubbed at the lipstick stain with my fingertip.

"Stop, okay? Don't make me feel as if I have to apologize all over again just because I happened to come over to see my grandchild."

"Honestly, I don't *want* you to feel that way." Wiping at the greasy smudge of scarlet on the coffee mug, I'd only succeeded in spreading it farther across the ceramic rim. "And actually, I've got work to do. I'm teaching two classes tomorrow."

"I'll just wait around awhile and finish up my coffee, and you get to work, Professor." Sherri raised herself from the couch and took the mug from me. "On second thought, if you've got some nail polish remover, I'll restore those nails of yours to their natural beauty."

"I'm a guy," I reminded her. "What would I be doing with nail polish remover?"

"Well, you'd better get some. You're not going to walk around like *that*, are you? You can't possibly go to school like that tomorrow."

"Don't worry about me."

"Oh, but I do," Sherri said. She stared me straight in the eye, and I had to look away. "It's kind of a lifelong habit."

"You'll get over it."

"Don't count on it," Sherri told me.

I didn't know whether to be pleased or insulted, and in my confusion left the room silently. Since Whitney-Rose was asleep in my study, I sank into an armchair in my bedroom, where I attacked my students' narratives with my micro-point green pen, correcting their spelling and careless grammar with growing exasperation, and questioning, in the margins, twists and turns of plot so implausible they made my teeth ache.

Slumping in my seat, I lowered my head to the chair's upholstered arm and contemplated a power nap—a fifteen-minute snooze from which I would awaken a new, improved man. I cradled my head in my arms and when I woke up, it was to the sound of my granddaughter's insistent cries, cries that suggested she wanted to be fed. And, too, that her diaper required my immediate attention.

"Sherri?" I called out hopefully.

But Sherri was already on her way to the Yale Club for

an exceptionally fine dinner, starting with a salad of baked goat cheese and mixed greens with raspberry vinegar and walnut oil, followed by a main course of broiled salmon in a caper and dill sauce, and then a slice of key lime pie that, she would later report back to me, could only be described as out of this world.

A Tupperware container of something or other in hand, Jessica Sarno, mother of Gabe and Nicole, stood, one evening a few weeks later, at my door. Barefoot. Bare-legged. Wrapped in a skimpy ice-blue satin robe. And all of thirty-two years old. Well, maybe thirty-five.

"For me? You shouldn't have," I teased as she handed me the Tupperware. "What's in there?"

"Hummus," Jessica said. "And sorry, but it's not for you. I'd open it myself but I just did my nails. See?"

"I see that it runs in the family, this business of manicures."

"They drain the life right out of me, those two little weasels," Jessica said. "But only sometimes." She had always struck me as a bit on the anorexic side; her pale arm, as she extended it toward me, looked awfully scrawny. Her eyes were the color of sea water—beautiful, really—her face drawn and unhappy. I'd overheard, while doing a load of sheets and towels in the laundry room one night, that Ron, her live-in boyfriend, had recently moved to Seattle for a new job and that she'd chosen to remain behind. One of the only things I could recall about the guy were those extra-large feet in burnished wing tips planted right next to mine in the elevator—size 13 or 14, I bet. And his job apparently required a spiffy suit and tie every day, so maybe he was a corporate lawyer or investment banker—just the kind of guy from whom I liked to keep my distance.

"That Gabriel is a very enterprising young man," I told Jessica. "Did he save up enough to get the *kidden* of his choice?"

"Got one from the ASPCA for free. And who do you think cleans out the litter box twice a day? Like I'm not busy enough as it is."

Snapping open the lid covering the hummus, I said, "Well, that's what parents are for, aren't they? For cleaning out litter boxes and lots of other fun things."

Jessica shrugged. "Could I come in for a minute, do you think? I could use a change of scenery."

"Are you sure it's safe to leave the kids?"

"No worries—they're in Brooklyn with their grandparents for an overnight."

"In that case, come on in." I'd rented a movie and my thumb had been poised to hit "play" when Jessica showed up. I didn't know her very well, but I could guess that with her boyfriend out of the picture, she was probably more than a little lonely and, possibly, bored. But the movie was due back at DVD World tomorrow and if I didn't start watching it soon, it would be too late.

"Would you like to watch a movie with me?"

"Sure, whatcha got?"

"Well, it's a foreign film about a woman and her retar—sorry—special needs sister. It's supposed to be excellent," I said, and then I broke the news that it was in Flemish. With subtitles, of course.

Jessica looked at me as if she couldn't believe what she was hearing. "Flemish?"

"It's what they speak in northern Belgium. And, um, a small section of northern France, I believe."

Shaking her head, smiling at me now, Jessica said accusingly, "Hey, you're a writer, aren't you? One of the neighbors told me. I mean, come on, who else would rent a movie in Flemish?"

"Well, it's true that I wrote some books a while ago."

"I started writing a book once," Jessica confessed. "I wrote six pages and I was so bummed, I just had to quit."

I offered her some sweet-and-savory popcorn straight from the bag. "What was it about?"

"Just the life and times of Jessica Sarno, I guess you could say. It was all basically true, which was probably why it was so fucking depressing."

"Tell me." The two of us were on separate love seats arranged perpendicular to one another; the TV screen was facing Jessica and I knew that we would never watch the movie—it just wasn't going to happen, in Flemish *or* English.

"Tell you *what?*" Jessica said.

"All about the life and times of Jessica Sarno."

"Really?"

"Why do you seem so surprised?" I asked her.

"Because whenever I wanted to talk, Ron wasn't in the mood to listen. Men never are."

"Well, this man is."

She considered this, then said, "Will you come and sit next to me?"

I got up and settled in beside her, telling myself she was simply one more student of mine needing an audience as she unburdened herself of whatever weight she'd been lugging around all too long. The only difference was that this was my living room and not a classroom, and that she was wearing a satin bathrobe and not much else. I found myself wishing she were fully dressed—bra, sweater, jeans, shoes, the works. I hadn't had what I would call meaningful sex in what felt like way too long; all I had were recent memories of one-night stands with women I'd met on OkCupid and—by mutual consent—never saw again afterward. My heart belonged to Sherri, but here was this young mother of two who needed me, or at least part of me, the part that would listen to her all night if necessary. I was a good listener—I never missed a word; every detail was of keen interest. It was a writerly habit of mine, life-long. And so you could always count on me to pay exquisitely close attention.

"Men," Jessica hissed.

"Pardon me?"

"Men are like parking spaces—the good ones are already taken and the ones that are left are handicapped."

"Is that a joke?"

"Not to me. Take Ron, for example," Jessica said, and put one hand into the popcorn. "Turns out he was cheating on me while I was pregnant with Nicole."

"Whoa! Jesus."

"People don't recover from something like that. They tell themselves they can, but it turns out they can't. They tell themselves the guy is garbage, pond scum. I mean, how could you love a man like that?"

"I have no idea. But I suppose it's possible."

"Sometimes I hate myself," Jessica said matter-of-factly. And then, "Could you put your arm around me or something, please?"

I could. She rested her head against my shoulder for a while; self-consciously, I patted her skinny wrist a few times. In my study, the baby slept undisturbed. On the Upper East Side, all the way across the Park, Sherri and her husband were in bed watching David Letterman. Or, perhaps, having the greatest sex of their lives.

Jessica Sarno took my hand and slipped it under the satin flap of her robe so I could savor the feel of her breast; try though I might, I couldn't for the life of me see a reason not to graciously accept the gift that was offered.

Eyes shut, my hand exploring Jessica, I remembered Sherri as she had been long ago, an impossibly young and hopeful bride, itching for things forever beyond my reach.

I could feel Jessica stirring beneath my hand now, could feel the confusion of my own beating heart. And when, a moment later, my granddaughter's sleep was interrupted by a couple of baby-demons and she let out what sounded like an anguished shriek, I hit the ground running and never looked back.

I was gone too long and after a while Jessica came looking for me. Together we stood over the Port-A-Crib, studying, in silent admiration, Whitney-Rose's blondish brows and snub nose.

"That's my granddaughter," I told Jessica proudly, but it didn't dissuade her; we both pretended I was young and suitable, just what she was looking for. We continued down the narrow hallway to my bedroom, me leading the way just a little uneasily, and Jessica following close behind. She opened her robe but never took it off, and afterward, as we lay on our backs in my untidy bed, on sheets that were overdue for a wash—neither of us saying a word as I politely arranged my arm around her—I could swear there was a tear or two of disappointment glimmering briefly in her eyes. It was only later, after I'd walked her to the front door and she padded home in her bare feet, that I realized she'd forgotten her hummus; that small plastic container which I eventually shoved to the back of my refrigerator and abandoned, forgetting, again and again, to return it to her.

And no matter how many times I waved to Nicole and Gabe frolicking in the hallway outside my apartment, they never once offered me another manicure.

Or even a single word about their kidden.

LOVED ONE

FOLLOWING THE DEATHS of their respective spouses, Daisy Jacobs and Spencer Wainwright happened to meet at a nonsectarian bereavement group that assembled once a week in a Jewish community center in Morningside Heights. Josh, Daisy's husband, had dozed off at the wheel while on a business trip near Cincinnati and had been killed instantly as his rented Buick collided with a massive oak tree. Daisy was home alone in their apartment enjoying the subtitles and subtext of a French comedy when, with some exasperation, she'd hit "pause" on the remote to answer the phone call bearing the devastating news. *She's devastated*, she heard friends whisper following the funeral—and she was, surely, brought to desolation by the violence of her grief. Several years earlier, she'd lost both her mother and her father in one awful twenty-two-month period, but that was different; they were people in their seventies, people who'd lived long enough to know they wouldn't be around forever. Gray-haired, slightly stooped, needing shots of cortisone to tame arthritis, Fosamax tablets to halt the progress of osteoporosis, her parents were claimed by heart disease and stroke and had the good fortune not to linger. But Josh's death—who could ever be prepared for that kind of sudden, senseless loss?

Daisy's college roommate and best friend, Elena, a child psychiatrist, prescribed Ativan for her so she could sleep at night, and although it was a blessing, it was also addictive and she gave it up after a few weeks. Ten months later her cat, Nelson, whom Daisy had brought to her marriage and truly adored, went into kidney failure and had to be put down. It was just too much, too much for a person to bear! Elena had been insisting for months that Daisy join a bereavement group, and now, just after Nelson's ashes had been buried—tucked inside a small cardboard box patterned with lilacs in Elena's suburban backyard—Daisy told herself that she just didn't have the strength to argue with her friend. Often, in fact, it seemed that she barely had the strength required to dress herself in the morning and go to work, but there was no question, economic or otherwise, of her staying home and licking her wounds all day. As weakened and fragile as she continued to feel, she understood it was imperative that she make the effort to get her act together, her life together. Posthaste. At thirty-eight, she was still young—or relatively young, she supposed, and relatively attractive. She believed her legs were too thin and shapeless, and thought her jaw too sharp, but her reddish-blond hair was silky, and her eyes were an unusually vivid green of the kind that often drew compliments. If her mother were alive, she would have pointed out, as she had many times, that Daisy had much to offer; if she shut her eyes in a quiet place and focused intently, Daisy could still feel her mother's expansiveness, still hear that warmest of voices extolling her virtues. Her mother, you could be sure, would have urged her to get herself over to the bereavement group even if Josh would have recommended that she stay home and read a good book instead—preferably one by Sartre or Kafka and not some bestselling self-help guru. A dozen years ago, Josh's cynicism and dark, mocking humor had won her over, and now that he was gone, one of the things Daisy missed most was that gift he'd had for cracking her up at singularly inappropriate moments: once, she had to bolt from a bar mitzvah service, wheezing with laughter (over what, she could no longer recall, though probably it had something to do with the bar mitzvah boy's girlish, nasal voice and his fierce-looking unibrow), her eyes and nose streaming, while Josh stayed behind, his face hidden in a prayer book, *his* laughter, at least, under control.

She shared this with the bereavement group at her very first meeting; surprisingly, she thought, several of the women listening wept as she spoke. Sitting in a circle of padded folding chairs, complimentary mini-bottles of Poland Spring arranged between their knees or in their laps, they stared at her—thirteen men and women, each of whom was intimately acquainted with the misery of fresh grief; the sort that brought you to your knees and made you wish, in all sincerity, for your own death.

"In a little while we're going to make a list of what we miss most about the loved ones we've lost, but first let's continue going around the room and introducing ourselves," said Helen, the group's leader. She was a sturdy, middle-aged woman with a tentative manner, brightly colored clothing, and a certificate in clinical social work, and she, too, had lost "a loved one," a term she seemed especially fond of. Her loss, however, dated back to the last century, to sometime in the mid-Nineties, which afforded her, she claimed, the kind of distance needed to help the rest of them huddled so pitifully in their circle of grief. Of all its members, the group learned, only Spencer Wainwright was in the odd position of having been divorced from his spouse at the time of her death, though he had moved back into their apartment to care for her in her final months. Daisy observed him closely as he struggled to examine his feelings for his ex-wife, who had fallen out of love with him for reasons that, eight months after her death, still remained a mystery to him. You had to admire his frankness, Daisy thought, knowing that she, certainly, could never publicly acknowledge that anyone had stopped loving her.

"Why torment yourself?" someone in the group asked Spencer. The guy was in a sweat-stained red T-shirt and had two purple tears tattooed down one cheek. "So she didn't love you, so what, dude. You're not a widower, you're just a divorced guy. What are you even doing here anyway? Go on the Internet or something and start dating again, dude."

Many in the group were nodding approvingly, and there was a lengthy debate about whether or not Spencer Wainwright actually deserved the official title of widower. A vote was taken and Helen counted the hands raised in the air. Spencer managed to squeak by in a vote of seven to five, but James, the man with the tattooed tears, sulked openly, mumbling under his breath to the man seated next to him.

"Please, guys," said Helen. "The majority has spoken and we're all going to give Spencer our enthusiastic support." She put her hand to her mouth and nipped worriedly at the tip of her pinky.

Seeing this, Daisy felt sorry for her. Helen was in over her head; if a show of hands were taken, Daisy wondered how many would argue with that. She stole a look at her watch, which had a shocking-pink leather band and a smiling chimp painted on the face, and which had turned out to be the last Valentine's gift she would ever receive from Josh. The meeting was only half over, but already she was champing at the bit. She looked over at Spencer Wainwright across from her in the circle; widower or divorcé, he was, unquestionably, the best-dressed man in the room, with his well-polished tasseled loafers, pressed khakis, and crewneck sweater in a dark shade of gray. He was an attractive guy, she thought, though not, of course, as appealing as Josh, who'd been born with what she liked to think of as a twinkle in his eye. She hated sentimentality of any stripe, but since she'd lost Josh, she allowed herself to savor a bit of it from time to time. (If mourning that twinkle was a touch sentimental, well, so be it.) Smiling at Spencer Wainwright now, she got his attention and the start of a smile, and then she immediately looked down into her lap at her mini-bottle of water, wondering if she'd been too forward.

At the end of the meeting, there was bitter coffee, and, heaped on flimsy paper plates, an assortment of ersatz Pepperidge Farm cookies, decidedly inferior to the real thing.

"I don't know, I'm having second thoughts about Oprah," said a woman named Bea who had a paperback copy of *The Sound and the Fury* protruding from a pocket of her handbag.

"Do you mean Oprah the show or Oprah the celebrity?" Daisy asked, only because Bea had grabbed hold of her upper arm and wouldn't let go. And also because Bea's son had thrown himself out a fourth-story window in New Haven, Connecticut, while under the influence of alcohol and cocaine and you couldn't ignore a woman like that when she was talking to you. Or could you? Daisy gently removed the woman's moist hand from her arm. "I'm so sorry about your son," she said.

"These cookies are sandy," someone else complained. "You know, like when you're at the beach on a windy day and everything you put into your mouth just tastes, well, gritty, I guess."

"I meant Oprah the show *and* Oprah the celebrity. She's the most powerful woman in the world," Bea said, "but I just think she needs to take it down a notch, and by that I—"

Spotting Spencer Wainwright sneaking out the door, Daisy excused herself from the conversation and hurried after him as he began walking down the empty hallway. "Wait!" she called out.

"Pardon me?" He turned to look at her and she could see—even in this scuffed hallway that could have used better lighting—that there were cookie crumbs caught in his beard.

"I just wanted to tell you," Daisy said, "that I think you have every right to consider yourself a widower. If that's your personal preference, I mean."

"Thank you."

In addition to the crumbs, there was some gray in his beard, which surprised her. He was probably in his early forties, she speculated, and wondered if he had kids at home who were, at this very instant, playing video or computer games with their babysitter. She hoped, though, that there were no children in the picture, because they would have been motherless, an undeniably cruel state.

"Well, thanks," said Spencer again, and gave a small wave goodbye.

"Wait!" How well did you have to know someone before you could tell him that there were crumbs nesting in his beard? Was ninety minutes long enough? "Hey," Daisy said, "I bet you had no idea I've been standing here admiring your beard, right?"

"What?" He seemed confused and she didn't blame him.

"It's a lovely dark brown, and very neatly groomed, except for the cookie crumbs, that is."

His hand went straight to his jaw. "Here?"

"Higher," said Daisy. "And a teensy bit to the left."

"Here?"

"Lower. And now a little to the right."

His cell phone rang. "I'll be home in about twenty minutes, okay, babydoll?" Spencer said when he answered it. He listened a while. "Maybe, maybe not, I don't know." He made kissing noises, and then closed the phone.

"So how old is Babydoll?" Daisy said, astonished at herself as she reached over and picked the crumbs deftly from his beard, as if she were using tweezers. What was she *doing*? He wasn't some child with a dirty face she happened to be babysitting—her little nephew, say, or Elena's son, Dakota—he was, in truth, a man she barely knew. And wasn't *she* a widow, someone who hadn't touched a man in nearly a year? What she had done about those crumbs was inexplicable, and she was mortified.

"Your daughter's not thirty-five, is she?" Daisy joked, the only way she could imagine to get past the deepest shame and embarrassment she'd felt in a long while.

It pleased her to hear Spencer laugh. "Not quite," he said.

"Is she old enough to read and write?" *Old enough to have attended her mother's funeral?*

"She's thirteen, but very petite. She's barely five feet."

"Hey, I'm a big five-two myself," said Daisy. "It's not the worst thing in the world." She couldn't stop herself from imagining Spencer at his wife's burial, his long fingers intertwined tightly with Babydoll's noticeably tiny ones as the coffin was lowered carefully into the earth. She herself would never go back to visit Josh's grave, a cold place that held nothing for her. At the cemetery on the single occasion she'd returned—when the gravestone was unveiled six months after Josh's death—she'd felt chilled inside and out, despite the mild, summery weather that morning at the end of May. It would have been comforting to believe in an afterlife, she knew, but no matter how she examined it, the notion struck her as a ludicrous one. If only she could embrace an image of Josh and her parents sitting down together companionably for some celestial feast at an all-you-can-eat Szechuan buffet in the kingdom of heaven!

"Not the worst thing in the world," Spencer agreed quietly.

Neither of them had anything to say after that, and when Spencer started for the exit, Daisy trailed behind him. He held the heavy door for her; outside, on the quiet side of the street, there was a lovely crescent of bright yellow moon waiting for them.

"Looks like a wedge of lemon up there," said Spencer. He sighed—a sigh of yearning, Daisy thought. "I love this city," he told her. They were walking toward Broadway now, only half a block away, where Columbia students were flocking to their favorite bars in the hopes of getting a buzz on. Daisy had gone to school here twenty years ago and had once known quite a bit about getting a buzz on. "Maybe I love it so much," Spencer continued, "because I grew up in the suburbs on a street called—and I kid you not—Cherry Vanilla Drive."

"No way!" said Daisy.

"And the next street over was Chocolate Ridge Road."

Daisy shook her head. "So you grew up on Cherry Vanilla Drive with heightened expectations about how sweet your life was going to be?"

Two men in kilts and thick white knee socks walked past them on Broadway. "He was in a para-type military organization," one of them said to the other. "An Aryan Nation-type thing."

"Fuck *that*!" said his companion.

"Expectations?" Spencer said. "The only expectation I had was that I would earn more money than my father ever did."

"Uh-huh," said Daisy. She felt herself blushing, as if he'd just confessed a passion for Internet porn or plain old ordinary hookers. So he'd had money on his mind even when he was a kid. *Weird!*

"And I'm happy to say that my expectation was met and then some."

"Thaaat's nice," Daisy said dismissively. She worked as an assistant director of Safe Haven, an organization that ran shelters for battered women all over the city. The big bucks would always elude her, but she had little trouble accepting that. "So what business are you in?" she asked Spencer. Through the plate glass window of a street-level gym, she observed a guy in a sleeveless sweatshirt and sweatpants studying himself in a mirrored wall as he juggled—very professionally—a trio of candlestick bowling pins. Or what looked like bowling pins. Daisy came to a stop so she could watch for a while.

"I'm an orthopedic surgeon in the largest orthopedic surgery practice in Brooklyn," Spencer told her.

"Wow!" said Daisy as the juggler increased his speed, bending on one knee now in an effort to keep everything flowing just right.

Misunderstanding, Spencer said, "Well, I do okay."

"That guy is really something," said Daisy. She walked up to the window, rapped on it sharply with two knuckles, caught the juggler's attention as he was taking a breather. Clapping her hands, she smiled and nodded as he bowed formally, acknowledging her applause.

On the sidewalk, Spencer waited for her. He looked a bit forlorn. "You'd think my father would have been proud of me getting my M.D.," he told her.

"What parent wouldn't be?"

"Forget the M.D.," said Spencer. "The one and only time he ever gave me a compliment was the day I installed an electric toothbrush in my parents' bathroom. I attached the mounting bracket to the wall with two Phillips-head screws and then clamped the base onto the bracket. And after I was done, my father stood there and said, 'Nice work, buddy.' Like I'd just finished a hip replacement or a ligament reconstruction."

"Is he still alive?"

"What? Oh yeah, he and my mother are in San Diego. Alive and well."

"Lucky you," said Daisy. She explained that she'd lost both her parents and that she still missed them. "Quite a lot, actually."

"Jesus," Spencer said. "So you're all alone in the world."

Daisy shrugged. She didn't like to think of herself that way, as someone who had sustained too many losses, someone who might be regarded with pity. She did, after all, have a job she cared a great deal about, a handful of friends she cherished, and a brother and sister-in-law, a nephew and two nieces. "I do okay," she said, and was startled when, in the next moment, Spencer took her hand.

"It's a rare person who would remove crumbs from a stranger's beard," he said, "and believe me, I'm well aware of that. Would you like a ride home?"

"I was going to take the subway at 116th Street and then the cross-town bus at 86th, so, yes, I'd love a ride home."

"There's my car right there." He pointed to a white Subaru, a modest car for a surgeon, Daisy noted. She was relieved to see he wasn't driving himself around in a Mercedes or BMW, show-offy cars that she was against on principle. That anyone would will-ingly fork over $50,000 or more for a single car offended her. Weren't there better ways to spend your money? She also dis-approved of people who ordered $300-per-person dinners and then raved about the magnificent food. Why not donate their money to Safe Haven instead? She thought of the women Safe Haven provided shelter for, women who had nowhere else to go to escape the dangerous men who had once loved them or claimed to love them still. She looked over at Spencer, settled behind the wheel of his Subaru now, and thought of the way he had taken her hand, so lightly, so unexpectedly. He must have been a devoted husband, she decided, and wondered why his wife had ditched him.

When they got to her building in Yorkville, he pulled into the circular driveway but kept the motor running. Since Babydoll was waiting for him, there was no point in inviting him up for a cup of better coffee, Daisy realized. She thanked him for the ride home and wondered what else she might say to him. She hadn't been on a date in twelve years—not that this was a date per se—and she'd forgotten the rhythm of the dance. "Well, see you next week," she chirped. Her fingers fooled with the door handle.

"*Def*initely," Spencer said.

He did not, however, show up at the next meeting of the bereavement group, though he appeared the week after, wearing precisely the same clothing he'd sported two weeks earlier. There was a very small, nearly imperceptible stain above one knee of his khakis, and a bit of dog or cat hair clinging to the front of his sweater. At coffee-and-dessert time, he told Daisy that Babydoll had been sick with a 24-hour bug. "Otherwise, I would have been here last week," he said. "I hope you realize that."

She was glad to hear this but wasn't sure if it was permis-sible to say so this early in the game. "Do you have a cat?" she asked hopefully.

"A Shih Tzu," he said. "I inherited him when my wife died,

and let me tell you, he's one huge pain in the ass."

"Tell me."

"Well," said Spencer, and took a dainty sip of undrink-able coffee, "yesterday I found him playing with a Lady Gillette disposable razor that he'd stolen from the garbage pail in the bathroom, and then later he got his paws on"—Spencer lowered his voice to a whisper—"a plastic tampon thing. He brought it to the kitchen and laid it at my daughter's feet like some kind of trophy. My wife would have been horribly embarrassed."

Ex-wife, Daisy thought. "My beloved cat, Nelson," she began, "is way too smart for that. He's smart enough to occasion-ally pee in the toilet in the guest bathroom, and to eat low-fat whipped cream from a demitasse spoon. He's amazing." Talking about Nelson in the present tense was a mistake; suddenly Daisy felt a sickening wave of grief wash over her and she had to sit down. She dropped into the nearest folding chair and cast her arm across her brow. Could it possibly have been the thought of Nelson that brought her to tears at this moment? She would never admit it to anyone, but Nelson's death had sometimes seemed the cruelest blow of all. Illness and a calamitous quirk of fate had taken her family from her, but couldn't the powers that be—whoever the fuck they were—have kept their greedy hands off the small, sweet cat who'd slept curled next to Daisy's ear every night for fourteen years? Couldn't they have left her *that*, at least? After Josh died, a well-meaning Safe Haven employee had sent Daisy a sympathy card with a quote, in embossed sil-very letters, from Einstein: *The Lord God is subtle but malicious he is not.*

Bull...shit! Daisy had shrieked in the privacy of her kitchen, tearing the card to shreds.

She could feel Spencer hovering nearby now, could feel his hand resting delicately on her shoulder.

"Can I take you home?" he said.

They slept together that night in the bed that had been hers and Josh's and had never been shared by anyone else, and for that, she wept soundlessly. Afterward, after Spencer had gone, she decided to bury, deep in her linen closet, Josh's pillow, upon which Spencer had innocently lowered his head. He was a gentle, quiet lover, so different from Josh, who had been energetic and talkative in bed, asking questions and giving orders and often making her laugh. She discovered that Spencer's legs and chest were nearly hairless, and this was a surprise to her; she was accustomed to the woolly feel of Josh's legs wrapped around her and to swirling her fingertips in the dark fur of his chest.

Sometimes, when Spencer slipped back into his clothes and went home to Babydoll, Daisy stayed in bed and indulged in a smidgen of self-pity, telling herself that Josh was irreplaceable and that she would continue, all the way through to the end of her life, to ache for him. *This sort of thinking just isn't in our best interest, guys*, she could hear Helen lecturing the bereavement group, and Daisy would have to admit that Helen—though not the sharpest knife in the drawer—did know a thing or two about what she repeatedly referred to as "the grief process." Daisy, on occasion, silently mocked Helen—her earnestness, her homely, Hush-Puppyish shoes, the way she literally wrung her hands when she talked. It occurred to Daisy that Josh would have found these things funny as well. But not Spencer, who would, she guessed, have thought it unkind to ridicule someone who was only trying to be helpful.

At the group's weekly meetings, she and Spencer always sat next to one another. Unthinkingly, Daisy would lean her head against his shoulder; absently, he would stroke her upturned palm with his thumb and bring it to his lips. They rarely spoke up to contribute anything of significance to the group but, instead, whispered together about things that had no connection whatsoever to the grief process. At the dessert-and-coffee table, they usually ignored both the miserable coffee and the dessert of the week and stood with their arms settled across each other's waists.

After nearly two months, Helen approached them one night just as the group was dispersing.

"Got a sec?" she said, but only after the room had emptied out. "We need to talk."

These words were familiar to Daisy, who had heard them once before, moments prior to being fired from her job behind the counter at Pizza Hut the summer between her sophomore and junior years at Columbia. (The reason for her dismissal was very specific: she was not, she was informed by the manager, "perky enough" for the job. *So what you're telling me is that if I perk the fuck up you'll let me keep working here?* Daisy had responded, collecting her backpack and sweater from where she'd stowed them under the counter. *One of the great moments of my life*, she told Josh years later, and even now, she still got a kick out of that small piece of her history. Out of that uncharacteristic insolence of hers.)

"Can't it wait until next week?" Spencer asked Helen. "It's just that I've got to get home to my kid." What he really meant, Daisy knew, was that he needed to go back to her apartment in Yorkville and help her out of her jeans.

Helen regarded them soberly. "I'm afraid not, guys," she said. "Why don't we sit down for a couple of minutes and talk this thing out."

"This thing?" said Daisy. *This thing* sounded ominous, she thought, but she wasn't sure what Helen had in mind.

Daisy and Spencer remained standing at the dessert table as Helen said, "Please don't take this the wrong way, guys, but I'm afraid you two just aren't bereft enough to…" She grasped her right wrist with her left hand and swiveled the wrist back and forth, stalling for time.

"Bereft enough to what?" Daisy said, though by now she suspected where this was going.

Helen couldn't bear to look at them, apparently. "It isn't that you're no longer welcome here," she said, staring at her graceless, oatmeal-colored shoes, "it's just that you're clearly no longer in need of our help."

"Hold it," said Spencer, "you're kicking us out of the group?"

"Oh, I wouldn't put such a negative spin on it," Helen said. She lifted her face to gaze at them apologetically. "Please don't be insulted. On the contrary, you should be flattered! You two have made significant progress in the grief process—in fact, I'd say you're at the head of the class. Valedictorian and salutatorian! Or even co-valedictorians! Congratulations to you both! And the best of luck to you."

Had Josh been at her side, Daisy would have hidden her face against his shoulder, shrieking with laughter. But here was Spencer, looking bemused and a little hurt, as if he'd been unjustly punished for some infraction he couldn't quite fathom.

"I'm not a psychiatrist," he told Helen, "but I *am* a physician, and, as such, I have to say that this, this"—he gestured with a flick of his wrist to the dessert table, and then to the empty folding chairs previously arranged in a neat circle and now just a shapeless mess—"this group you're in charge of is being run in a highly unprofessional manner."

It was Helen's turn to look hurt. "Well, I'm sorry you feel that way," she said, her voice so trembly it seemed she was about to cry. "I do my best, week after week, and not once have I ever heard a single complaint from anyone…except on the subject of *you* guys."

"What do you mean?" said Daisy. Her face was blazing; she imagined the group regressing, en masse, to a miserable adolescence, gossiping sourly about her in a vast, rank-smelling high school cafeteria as a pair of female teachers on lunch duty tried to listen in.

"I'd rather not get into the nitty-gritty of it, but what I *will* say is that I've received a number of late-night phone calls asking for your…expulsion." Helen appeared, suddenly, more in control, and the possibility of tears being shed now seemed remote.

Seizing Daisy by the tip of her thumb, Spencer murmured, "Let's get out of here."

"You can wait for me in the car," she told him, and swiftly reclaimed her thumb.

"If you're staying, I'm staying," he said, though this sounded halfhearted, as if he were reluctantly doing her a favor.

She might have been a widow and an orphan, but she didn't, in fact, need favors from anyone. "Out with it, please," she told Helen.

"All right, listen," Helen said, "you guys show up here every week all misty-eyed, everyone assumes you're probably sleeping together, and frankly, it's bad for morale around here. There's a sense of common purpose in this room, an *esprit de corps*, if you will, and you two are someplace else. Pursuing your own agenda, as it were."

"It's a free country, last time I checked," Spencer pointed out. "And anyway, whose business is it if we're sleeping together?"

"*As it were*," Daisy said, already giggly. She knew exactly what Josh would have found most hilarious, knew that he would have taken particular pleasure in Helen's *esprit de corps, if you will*. And she heard herself bringing forth great whoops of laughter now, celebrating the memory of her one and only marriage, which had been far too brief, and which was, she understood in her marrow, irretrievable.

"What's so funny?" Spencer said. "*What?*" he said as Daisy continued to laugh.

How could she possibly explain? Her shoulders heaved with laughter; her stomach ached with it. She wished she had something to offer—a parting gift of a well-chosen word or two—but nothing came to her.

"For crying out loud, what *is* it?" said Spencer. He and Helen were gaping at her as if she were deranged; really, Daisy thought, who could blame them?

Spencer had her by the elbow now; still laughing, she shook him off as easily and impatiently as if he were a tiny, harmless spider caught in her hair. Eyes closed, it was Josh she could see combing through it, again and again, the blunt tips of his heartbreakingly soft-skinned fingers coming to rest, at last, in the warm, velveteen crook of her arm.

SPARKLE

THE TWINS, Amber and Brianna, are sixteen. They dress for school all in black, including twenty-eyelet, over-the-knee boots with thick rubber soles and tight-fitting leather jackets with zippered sleeves. In spring and summer, the jackets are gone, and in their place are T-shirts that barely cover the girls' midriffs and expose the little tattoos of red hearts flanked by bat wings on the delicate flesh of their pale inner arms. *Why all that black? Are you kids in mourning?* Grace wants to ask, but does not, because she is, after all, only their aunt and not on top of the goth/vampire/punk fashion scene for teens. And, too, the twins' mother and father might return at any moment to reclaim them, and Grace surely doesn't want it said that she's been anything but loving and loyal.

The condo their father shares with his lover and her two young sons is just under an hour from Grace's small tract house in Nassau County, where the twins have been living for the past three years, ever since their mother went AWOL. Wayne, their father, calls them around the first and fifteenth of each month wanting to know if they need anything, and with great exasperation in their voices, they always tell him no. This afternoon, though, Wayne shows up bearing gifts from Rockbottom, a discount drugstore: bottles of expensive designer shampoo, two mini-sized hair dryers that fold up to fit into the palm of your hand, and packages of tiny soaps shaped like ballet slippers, angel fish, smiling dolphins, and naked infants in three colors—pink, dark-brown, and tan.

"I'm thinking those hair dryers are kinda cute," Brianna says. "But honestly? We were sorta hoping for new iPods. The screen on mine is cracked, and Amber's hard drive died or something." Under the kitchen's unflattering fluorescent lighting, Brianna's skin looks morbidly pale from the baby powder she routinely dusts across her face and throat; black eye shadow and thick liner and a slash of none-too-subtle black lipstick contrast starkly with her carefully applied pallor. Amber, unsurprisingly, looks exactly the same, except for the dramatic rings of dark-blue shadow she sports around her eyes. When asked *why* the baby powder-pale look, the twins will instantly offer up, with all sincerity and often in unison, *Oh, we just totally like celebrating the beauty of death, okay?* Why they're permitted by the principal to attend class looking like punked-out goth vampires is one of the mysteries Grace is free to contemplate whenever she likes.

Amber tugs at her father's shirt sleeve now, displaying the chipped black polish on all five fingers of her hand. "Are you for real?" she says. "You bring us these totally random presents from a drugstore? A *discount* drugstore? I mean, why bother to give us anything at all? What are you trying to do?"

Wayne looks puzzled. "What do you mean? I love you guys," he says, and drapes an arm around each of them. "With all my, um, heart..."

"I'm really impressed," Amber says. She slips out from under his arm, and, a minute later, slams into the bedroom she shares with Brianna at the other end of the house.

Removing her father's hand from her shoulder, Brianna

raises his arm and spins herself away from him. "You are totally pathetic, *Wayne*," she announces, and then she vanishes.

"Teenagers," Wayne says, sighing, as if that were all that were needed to let him off the hook. Now he's glaring in Grace's direction. "And what's up with those scary haircuts?" he says. "The girls look like they were in an accident or something. Why didn't you talk them out of it?"

"They're sixteen," Grace informs her brother. "Have you ever tried to talk a sixteen-year-old into or out of *anything*?" But she has to admit he does have a point—when the girls returned home from Kutting Kraze yesterday, bursts of their naturally dark hair dyed an odd terra-cotta and cut in short, choppy, deliberately uneven layers—as if by a drunken or stoned hairstylist—she'd wanted to cry. (The $150 charged to her Mastercard didn't lift her spirits much, either.) Later, after the twins went into the bathroom and added some product, their hair stood out on end as if they'd just received the shock of their young lives.

Wayne slowly pulls out his wallet from the rear pocket of his jeans and hands Grace a check, the one he writes out in her name at the beginning of every month. "Little kids are hard, too," he says. "It's no picnic being a stepfather or whatever to Nicholas and Jeremy."

Without her drugstore reading glasses, Grace has to hold out the check at arm's length in order to see what's what. She finds herself, yet again, contemplating her soon-to-be official status as a middle-aged person. At this stage of the game, with her fortieth birthday out there on the horizon, she should be hitting some of those sites on the Internet—maybe eHarmony or PlentyofFish.com. The truth is, she's been alone for too long. And way too busy earning a living and raising somebody else's moody, slightly scary-looking teenagers. Amber's infected belly button piercing (in frightening proximity to her fallopian tubes!), Brianna's brand new "LOVE SUX" tattoo on her lower back, the 65 in geometry circled in her homeroom teacher's red pen on her most recent report card signifying Brianna had come *this* close to failing; all of this is a lot to handle for Grace, who, at this moment, would like to point out to Wayne that she isn't even the twins' legal guardian.

"I'm already in the market for bifocals or progressive lenses or whatever they call them," she confesses. "Before you know it, my memory will start to fail and the girls will take advantage of me even more than they do now. Soon they'll be asking for a trip to the gynecologist and a prescription for the pill and I won't know what my answer should be. I'll probably be wringing my hands and thinking about shooting myself."

"*You?*" Wayne says in a soft voice. He stares at her as if she's wounded him. "Not you, Gracie."

"Yes, *me*," she says. "And it strikes me at least once a day that I'm not particularly well-suited for this foster parent business." She folds his check, over and over again, until it's the size of a piece of the bubble gum the girls are always chewing so energetically and then jamming under the kitchen table just for fun. "Are you listening to me, Wayne?" she asks him. "Are you paying attention?"

"That reminds me," Wayne says, and he removes a small, glossy white cardboard box from his shirt pocket. Opening it himself, he extracts the thin chain of a necklace with the words "#1 Aunt"—all in Florentine gold—suspended from it.

"It's a handsome piece of jewelry," Grace says, "but unfortunately, it doesn't change a thing." *A fucking thing*, she almost says but does not. Gazing at him, at his softly alluring brown eyes, the thick, bronze-colored beard that half-conceals the corners of his mouth, she can't help but feel a quiver of pleasure in the knowledge that this baby brother of hers, four years younger, is still a good-looking guy, a hottie, as her nieces would say. (Though not about *him*, of course.) Women—his ex-wife, Callie, and the girlfriends thereafter—had usually mistaken his handsomeness for goodness and also for the promise of happiness. He and Callie had met only months after high school, at a time when, more than anything, he liked to drive his Mazda

RX-7 convertible on the back roads out on the North Shore. Especially at night, with Callie beside him, wearing a little too much perfume and the shortest, tightest fake-leather skirt imaginable. Although they'd barely been eighteen, Callie—who had no plans to go to college and was working full-time as a sales associate in the women's apparel department at Sears—had been fantasizing aloud about marriage. She wanted to have children and live with Wayne in a place of their own; even at eighteen, it was all she could envision for herself. Wayne managed to finish two semesters at Suffolk Community College, where he half-heartedly enrolled in some business courses—on a campus that was formerly a sanitarium for TB patients—and then he and Callie were married, because, Grace always suspected, Wayne hadn't the slightest idea *what* he wanted. (Of course, marriages often happened that way, she knew—one person had an idea in her head and the other person just sank into the comfortable seat that had been offered him.) The twins were born soon afterward, and from the start, Callie had her hands full; her own parents had moved from Long Island to a suburb of Cleveland, too far to be of any help, and her in-laws, Grace's parents, had moved to Cape Coral, Florida, because of her father's asthma. Those first few years, Callie seemed close to a meltdown whenever Grace stopped by to see her. According to Callie, the twins were terrible sleepers and terrible eaters; just impossible kids. They intentionally peed on the bathroom floor, an inch or two from the toilet bowl, wrecked the volume on the TV remote, gleefully shredded magazines and newspapers into confetti. "Children are children," Grace told her, though after five years of marriage, she still didn't have any of her own. (And would, a year later, find herself divorced from the husband with whom she'd mistakenly believed herself to be in love from almost the moment they met, working together in risk management at a local hospital.) "What did you *expect?*" Grace asked Callie, her voice edged with impatience. "That they'd be perfectly formed miniature adults, born fully toilet-trained and with beautiful table manners?"

Sometimes when Grace dropped by for a visit in the middle of a Saturday afternoon, the tiny house Wayne and his young family were living in was scented with the funk of recently enjoyed weed. It helped her relax, Callie explained once, looking so exhausted and bemused that Grace cast her arms around her sister-in-law's narrow shoulders and pressed against her fiercely, as if, at that moment, there were the most poignant love between them. She extracted a promise from Callie to cut out all that pot smoking; after that, the house smelled of Glade French Vanilla, and Callie seemed as confused as she always had. But Grace could see for herself that the girls were thriving, even though two-thirds of their daily meals consisted of a veneer of tuna fish pressed between two slices of American cheese and cut into four equal triangles.

In those days, Grace remembers, her brother claimed that the twins were the greatest pleasure of his life and that he would kill himself if anything ever happened to them. If only he'd felt the same about Callie. "You're digging a grave for that marriage of yours," Grace warned him whenever he confided in her, but he didn't seem concerned in the slightest. His faithlessness was the one thing Callie could count on. She'd married a man other women always had their eye on—a man easily flattered and not given to much thought. It was Grace's theory that Callie looked the other way or deliberately saw everything in a blur, refusing to let herself take in all the little particulars of Wayne's betrayals. Or maybe, Grace thought, Callie had just been waiting for the right moment to make her move.

That turned out to be the morning after the twins' pajama party in honor of their thirteenth birthday. The last guest had gone home, and Callie did a thorough clean-up of the house, as if, Wayne confided, to ensure that years later no one could accuse her of having left behind a mess. She kissed him and the twins goodbye, and drove off in her old Honda station wagon adorned with the bumper sticker that said "MOM'S TAXI" in letters that glowed in the dark.

Wayne was distraught when he realized that her urgent trip to CVS for a box of Tampax was, in fact, a fabrication, and that she was gone for good, immediately moving in with a divorced friend she'd known since childhood, who found her a job as a receptionist at a fitness club in the city. Unburdening himself to Grace, Wayne told her that he phoned Callie incessantly and sent a blizzard of apologetic emails and texts, along with gift baskets from Edible Arrangements full of pineapple, cantaloupe, and honeydew, all carved into the shape of flowers. He'd made a jolting discovery, he said; after fourteen years of marriage to Callie, it finally occurred to him that he actually loved her, wanted her, needed her. All of which sounded to Grace like the insipid lyrics of a truly uninspiring country-Western song.

According to Wayne, Callie's response was an indifferent "Coulda fooled me," though she did make a point of thanking him for all his gifts, most notably the chocolate-covered strawberries from Edible Arrangements, and the basket with the imported cheeses and crackers. "Oh yeah, and the brie was excellent," she reported.

"Look, you have two kids who need taking care of, and you've got to get your act together, Wayne," Grace advised him, but he merely looked at her, nettled, as if all she'd given him was useless information.

Being a single parent wasn't for him; he didn't have much more than the vaguest notion of how to keep his thirteen-year-olds in line. And when it came to keeping them happy? *I got nothin',* he told Grace. *No ideas at all.* Whatever he said to them was wrong wrong wrong, usually the exact opposite of what they wanted to hear. The three of them were miserable together and every day was worse than the last, he complained to Grace. There weren't any grandparents to help out: what was he supposed to do, put the twins up for adoption?

"Of course not," Grace said warily. "Is that a joke?"

Wasn't she the one who worked her way through college as a part-time nanny? And hadn't she always been a people person?

Wayne reminded her.

"So everyone tells me," she said.

Brianna and Amber stayed with her from then on, and it was as if there were nothing more natural in the world than for the three of them to have fallen in place like that. In the beginning, there were occasional phone calls and emails from Callie, a few belated birthday cards, a couple of plans for visits that fell through at the last minute—the usual perfunctory gestures from someone who cared, though not enough. Then Callie phoned to inform Grace that she was moving away and that the girls wouldn't be hearing from her again. As she saw it, they were better off hearing nothing from her than the little she had to offer. "Why confuse them?" she said. "The truth is they're motherless, but at least they have *you*."

Grace wanted to say that they were practically fatherless, too, since Wayne had moved in with his girlfriend, Deb, and her two little boys—less than six months after Callie left him—and only showed up to see his daughters when he got the urge, which wasn't often. "You need to get yourself over here and take those kids, Callie," Grace whispered into the phone, thinking there was still a chance her sister-in-law might have a change of heart. "I mean, really—it's like I'm running a home for orphans here." But there was no response from Callie, who evidently felt no compunction about hanging up on her, mid-conversation. And absenting herself from her children's lives with very little effort, it seemed.

Lifting her hands to the back of her neck now, Grace fastens the gold necklace from Wayne and saunters into the bathroom to study herself in the mirror. What she sees is someone in need of a makeover—new, brighter hair color; new, tighter skin around the eyes and mouth and throat; new goddamn *life*. She remembers her grandfather's murmured words, years ago, only a few hours before he died: *Enough is enough*, he'd told the family members assembled at his bedside, and of course, Grace thinks as she unclasps the necklace proclaiming her status as #1 Aunt, he was undeniably right.

She makes her way back into the kitchen, the necklace cupped in her hand in a brilliant heap. She places it carefully on the table, where it glitters under the fluorescent light.

"No dice," she says. "I love those girls as if they were my own, but it's still no dice."

"I thought they were your joy and your heartache," Wayne says, quoting her accurately enough. He frowns at the necklace, but leaves it untouched on the table.

"I don't think so," Grace says. She stares straight at him. "It's time for you to man up, Wayne. And this time I really mean it."

She listens to him tell her that he needs time to find a house big enough for all four kids; it will be a wonderful house, he promises, a black-and-white colonial set far back from the road, nearly hidden behind a stand of old oaks. A house like the ones on the North Shore he used to drive past in his Mazda, Callie nestled beside him, her head tilted sweetly against his shoulder, all those years ago before the twins were born. "All those years ago," he repeats, and then leans across the table, necklace in hand.

"Come on," he insists. "Just take the necklace. I mean, why can't you let me do this one thing for you, Gracie?"

In the six months Wayne has been searching for a house, he hasn't come across a single one that thrills him and which, at the same time, is affordable on his salary as a salesman in the Audi dealership owned by an old high school friend of his. But he isn't giving up. Somewhere out there, he promises Grace, there's a house he'll fall in love with, a house where he'll want to spend the rest of his life.

More modest expectations would probably help, Grace thinks, but keeps it to herself, not wanting to offend him.

"Will you just find a house, for Christ's sake! You don't

have to fucking marry it! All you have to do is put down your goddamn twenty percent!" she shouts into the phone late one night when, yet again, Wayne is wasting time bemoaning the general crappy quality of the few houses he can afford.

Before hanging up, Grace apologizes for cursing.

"No worries," Wayne says.

———

These days, unaccountably, the twins want to look like Madonna in her old music videos from the Eighties. They wear dog collars around their slender wrists; crucifixes on strands of black plastic pearls dangle to their navels. Their hair is a different garish color every month; this month it's a pinkish-purple. "I love you but you're looking awfully trashy," Grace tells them, feeling drained and helpless. When her repeated accusations of trashiness fail to do the trick, she tells them that *People* magazine regularly put Madonna on its worst-dressed list. The girls aren't impressed by that, either.

One Sunday afternoon, as Grace stands in the kitchen sorting the twins' laundry into piles of dark and light, her friend Lou Ann calls, all heated up, with the news that she's just seen Callie.

"Are you sure?" Grace says. Over the years, she'd heard reports that Callie had been spotted farther out on the Island, once in a Price Chopper in Huntington, and another time, last summer, on the beach in Northport, looking terrific in an eye-catching bikini. Both times Grace tried to get Wayne to track her down, but clearly he'd lost interest, and why not, Grace thought—he had his girlfriend Deb to keep him warm and he had *her* to keep his children safe and cozy.

"Are you sure?" she repeats.

"She had on a cowboy hat, but it was Callie all right," Lou Ann insists. "She's working behind the counter of the Roy Rogers all the way out near the Brookhaven airport. She took my order very politely but pretended not to know me. I stared at her and she stared at the floor and finally I got so furious I leaned over the counter and said, 'How dare you let your husband dump your precious children with your sister-in-law like that! Who the hell do you think you are? What's WRONG with you?'"

"How mortifying," Grace says, feeling sorry for Callie in spite of herself. She tries to conjure up an image of Callie dressed for work in a cowboy hat, her light hair in braids reaching to her shoulders, a few freckles drawn on her nose with eyebrow pencil. At this moment, she can only remember Callie as a teenager, a thin little girl in a vinyl mini-skirt, someone who was soft-spoken and didn't smile easily, with her head turned toward her shoulder, eyes lowered, as if she were uncertain of her own words; someone who might be in danger of falling to pieces if she knew what her Madonna-adoring children looked like now.

Grace is standing out in the cold near the entrance to Roy Rogers, her heart thumping, when she's approached by someone dressed in a filthy, blood-red running suit. "Can you spare forty-six cents?" the man says.

"I'm sorry, *what*?"

"It's for an order of cole slaw, what did you think?" the man answers, in a voice that's filled with contempt for her.

Silently Grace hands him two quarters, both of which slip through his trembling fingers and fall into the island of frozen grass at their feet. He moves with heartrending swiftness, and, in an instant, is down on his hands and knees in search of the coins. "Thanks a lot, *you*," he says fiercely, not bothering to raise his head to look at her.

Grace hurries into the restaurant, too angry and upset to help him. She passes through an empty wooden corral set up for customers waiting in line, and marches resolutely up to the counter. It's almost four o'clock. She's the only customer waiting, though there are some teenagers clowning around at the condiments bar and a handful of people seated at tables, bent over their plastic trays of Double R Bar burgers and Gold Rush chicken sandwiches. Posted over the entranceway to the restrooms is what looks like an authentic pair of cattle horns, and on one wall a large painting of Roy Rogers and Trigger is hung in a wide, gilt-edged frame.

"Howdy pardner," the young guy waiting to take her order says. "And what'll it be today?"

"I'm just here to see Callie," Grace says. "Do you know her?"

"Don't think so." The kid, probably still a teenager, plays with the official Roy Rogers bandanna tied at his neck. "What does she look like?"

"Well, she's small and thin, talks kind of quietly…"

"You mean Sparkle," the kid says. He disappears into the back, and a few moments later she's face to face with her sister-in-law. It's been three years; she wonders if Callie has been keeping track.

"Well, look at *you*," Grace says. For some reason, tears spring to her eyes. She reaches over and tips back Callie's cowboy hat with one finger.

Callie takes a single step away from the counter. She hesitates, then leans forward and plants a modest, silent kiss on Grace's cheek.

"Can I take your order?" she says impassively.

"You bet," Grace says. She studies the menu board, but she's still teary-eyed and the words look a little blurry and confusing. "I'll have a Filet-O-Fish sandwich and a medium coffee, light."

"Actually, that's McDonald's," Callie says.

"What?"

"It's just that you can't order fish here."

Grace turns to stare at the painting of Roy Rogers, who's bent on one knee gazing at the mountains rising in the background while Trigger drinks from a sky-blue watering hole. "Callie," she begins, "you've got to help me."

"*Sparkle*," Callie corrects her, tapping the plastic name badge above the pocket of her uniform.

"What's *that* supposed to mean?"

"I changed my name to Sparkle," Callie announces. "I mean, Drew, my boyfriend, did."

"Well, listen…Sparkle," Grace says, "you've got to start acting like a mother to your kids again, do you get that?"

"He says I light up his life," Callie reports, without even a whiff of irony, Grace notes sadly. "I haven't told him about my kids. It's too soon for that yet—we've only been seeing each other for a couple of months." She comes around to Grace's side of the counter and leads her to a drafty table way in back, near the door. "Things are happening, but I'm not sure what," she says. "We may be getting married or buying a condo, maybe both, I just don't know." Taking a paper napkin from the pocket of her apron, she thoughtfully brushes an errant French fry off a seat meant for Grace. "You can sit down now," she says.

"Not here."

"How about a booth?"

"I want to talk to you," Grace says, "but not like this, not at Roy Rogers."

"My shift is over anyway. Let me change my clothes and I'll be right back."

While she's gone, Grace looks into a store window across the small parking lot and sees a woman trimming the bangs on a little girl mannequin. *Not too short*, Grace wants to say. The woman lets the hair fall into her palm. She sweeps some away from the mannequin's cheek with her fingertips. She straightens the shirt collar at the mannequin's shoulders, then pats it on the behind. Then she darts out of the window and back into the store. Watching her, Grace thinks, *She* must be somebody's mother. She thinks how long it's been since Callie's hands passed so gently, so affectionately, across the soft faces of her daughters. She thinks of Wayne spending all his time with someone else's children in a house that, like the perfect house of his dreams, will

141

never have enough space for all of them.

"I've gotta be at the gym at five o'clock," Callie is saying, "and I can't cancel because my trainer's waiting for me. But do you wanna walk with me to my car?" She's wearing a big, stretched-out sweater with a quartet of surprisingly gloomy-looking teddy bears across the middle, surrounded by rows of bleached-out pink hearts.

"That sweater of yours looks like something the twins haven't worn since they were in kindergarten," Grace observes, as they leave the restaurant and walk through the parking lot together to Callie's car. "You should see their tattoos. I mean, they wouldn't touch a teddy bear sweater if their lives depended on it."

"Tattoos?" says Callie, and smiles briefly. "It's just too hard to think of them that way—as teenagers, I mean. I never do." She studies her manicured hand, lying so still across the polished silvery hood of her Altima. "In my dreams," she says, "they're always babies, maybe nine months old or so, watching me from their playpen while I get their dinner ready. I'm smoking a joint and heating up jars of baby food in the microwave. Wayne's not coming home for dinner because he's out with one of his girlfriends but that's all right because I'm a little bit high and at least I've got company—two little babies who smile at me deliciously from inside their playpen. They're not gonna eat the dinner I'm heating up and they're not gonna go to sleep, they're just gonna sit there in their diapers and overalls and smile at their idiot mother who can't think of what else to do except smile back at them."

"Oh, Callie," Grace says, her voice whispery.

"*Sparkle*," she says. "Drew keeps telling me I've gotta be firm about that."

Grace can see Callie's sigh, a small white cloud of smoke in the frozen air. She reaches out an arm to capture it, and imagines the soft feel of it against her hand.

Months later, toward the end of summer, she gets a card—snail mail—from Callie, inviting her to lunch. The invitation has tiny martini glasses and bits of confetti scattered along the front; opening it, Grace sees that Callie has crossed out the line at the top that says "We're Having a Party!"; "PLEASE come for lunch" is handwritten above it, each letter of the "please" printed in multi-colored glitter. Grace doesn't tell anyone about the invitation and doesn't bother to call Callie; she RSVPs with a three-word email.

She shows up at Callie's place precisely on time, carrying a quartet of homemade cupcakes with cream cheese frosting in a bakery box. The new duplex condo where Callie lives is on the same property where, many years ago, the twins attended the Red Robin day camp, run by a bossy blonde with whom Wayne had a brief affair. Each unit has its own pocket-sized yard, most of them cluttered with barbecues, Radio Flyer tricycles, doll strollers occupied by abandoned Ernies and Berts and wide-faced Hello Kitty plush toys. Callie's yard is empty except for a gas grill, its cover a copper helmet gleaming extravagantly in the sunlight.

When Callie answers the door, she's wearing a sleeveless black scoop-necked dress, high-heeled sandals, and a triple strand of pearls. Her cheekbones are bright with blush-on, her eyes delicately outlined in black. "I knew you'd be here right on time," she says. "Thank you for that."

"I feel awful," Grace says, gesturing toward her capri pants and flip-flops; at least she had a pedicure before the weekend. But who, she wonders, is Callie trying to impress? "I had no idea this was going to be so formal," she says.

"Don't be silly," Callie says. "Come and sit down."

Grace walks guardedly across the hardwood floor, which she sees has been pickled a grayish white and is absolutely spotless. She seats herself at the edge of an enormous U-shaped sectional couch that seems to go on forever. There's a fifty-inch flat-screen TV—the largest she's ever seen in someone's home—opposite the leather couch, and a wall of vertical Levolors in a color Callie says is called "Honey Suckle."

"Nice," Grace says.

"Yeah, and the blinds in the bedrooms are these beautiful colors Oregano and Peach Daiquiri," Callie tells her, smiling. "But we just moved in last month, and of course we're planning to do a lot more with this place. We're installing a hot tub and sauna in the master bath and redoing all the counters and floors—all three baths and the kitchen—in marble. It's gonna be pretty awesome, I think."

If you say so. "And who's 'we'?"

"Oh, sorry, I meant my boyfriend, Drew."

"I remember," Grace says. She clears her throat. "The one who said you light up his life. So what does he do for a living?"

"He's a professional," Callie says proudly. "An optometrist."

Grace nods. "So how are things going at Roy Rogers?"

"Been there, done that," Callie says. "I'm working with Drew now as his assistant. I help people choose their frames and get comfortable with them. And when we're ready to close up, I vacuum a little, Windex all the mirrors…It's nice—we have lunch together every day."

"Could I possibly have a drink?" Grace asks. She gets up and stands at the window, parting the Levolors and staining their gleaming surface with her fingertips. In the parking lot two stories below, a man in a black yarmulke with a motorcycle helmet under his arm squats near his Kawasaki and talks to a little girl wearing a frilly party dress.

"Is this okay?" Callie says, handing Grace a glass of Chardonnay; Grace can see the $4.69 price sticker from Target ornamenting the bottle that rests on the counter. "Why don't we get started on lunch."

"I'm actually not that hungry," Grace says, but she allows herself to be seated at the head of the dining-room table, where Callie serves her a narrow triangle of what she identifies as spinach-and-mushroom pie. As Grace is finishing her wine, a husky, cinnamon-colored cat without a tail vaults onto the table. "What happened to *you*, you poor thing?" she says after Callie removes the cat and returns him to the floor.

"No no, he's a Manx, he's fine. It's just that he was late getting into the ark and Noah slammed the door shut on his tail," Callie says nonchalantly.

"Is it possible I'm drunk on one glass of wine?" Grace muses. "Did you just say something about Noah's ark?"

"Kidding! But I think it might be part of a story in the bible."

Grace picks up her empty wine glass, peers into it and places it back on the table. "It's wonderful…this life you've made for yourself…"

"That's right," Callie agrees. "I'm into Life Three now. Lives One and Two are over, thank God—I still can't believe I survived them. And now that I'm in Life Three, I can take the girls back. I know it's been such a long time, like, forever, really, but I'm finally there. And Drew says it's all right, he's sure I can handle it."

Grace feels herself stiffen. "So this is Life Three? Does this have anything to do with reincarnation? Like Alan Arkin, from *Little Miss Sunshine*, you know who I mean? I read somewhere that he's convinced he had an earlier life in the 18th century and that he was guillotined in the French Revolution." She leans over the table and takes Callie's hand. "So what happened in Lives One and Two? Please don't tell me you were Marie Antoinette."

"Life One," says Callie, pulling her hand away, "was Wayne. You know all about *that* disaster. Life Two was mostly on my own, and basically a mess, but definitely an improvement over Life One. Life Three is Drew," she says. She smiles shyly. "And believe me, there's more than enough room in Life Three for my kids. It's got space that's just waiting to be filled by them."

"They're sixteen," Grace reminds her. "I don't think you have a clue what that means." Her heart is pulsing like mad, and she has to put her palm to her chest to muffle the commotion.

"I'm their mother," Callie says. "I'll figure it out."

"I wouldn't be so quick to jump to conclusions, Callie."

"*Sparkle*," Callie says. "Please."

"Well, here's *my* life, *Sparkle*: it seems like I have to text the twins every two minutes because they never answer their cell phones when they're out late. And they only text me back when they feel like it. It makes me crazy," Grace reports. "And Brianna has a new boyfriend who tosses his used condoms into the garbage pail in the bathroom where, I guess, he thinks I'm not going to find them."

Hearing this, Callie doesn't bat a heavily mascaraed eyelash. "Trust me, I can handle it," she says, sounding impatient, and much too sure of herself, Grace thinks.

"It's not what anyone would call an easy job," Grace says soberly. "It's no joke."

"I'm a grown-up," Callie says, as if to set the record straight. "I can take it, I promise you."

Yeah, sure. Grace snickers. "Sorry," she says.

"God knows, I wasn't anything like a grown-up when I married Wayne, I get that."

"You can't have them back," Grace hears someone saying. She blinks her eyes in astonishment, then says, "No way I'm going to hand them over to someone who thinks she's got nine lives."

"This is Life Three and it's gonna last forever," Callie says, her voice dreamy. She yanks open a drawer on the sideboard next to her, removes a tube of peppermint ChapStick, and absently applies it to her lips. "Didn't you hear me? Everything's going right, finally. Anyway, you're ready for a Life Three of your own, kiddo." She's out of her seat now, and hurries around to Grace. "It's what you've been wanting all along," she says. Kneeling in front of Grace, Callie raises her hands and grips the arms of the chair. "Look, you're not much different from me," she says in a soothing voice. "Things happen and you pretend they're nothing out of the ordinary, that somehow you'll get by. But really they're so outrageous, so completely wrong, that even a stranger on the street can see what a fool you've been."

Callie tells her how happy the twins will be living in a home with a 3-D Blu-ray player and DVRs in every room. "Three-D movies in your own home, how cool is that? That's Drew, top of the line all the way," Callie assures her.

"Even so," Grace says, "you can't have them back." She imagines herself on both the local news and CNN, poised dramatically on the steps of the Nassau County courthouse, dressed in an expensive cashmere coat, speaking in a clear, direct voice that mesmerizes everyone in earshot.

They are my joy and my heartache, she says calmly into the shining bouquet of microphones held up to her lips.

Sparkle is already shaking her head *no*, worrying the fake pearls at her long, pale throat over and over again, mistaking them for rosary beads and counting her prayers.

HASTA LUEGO

HAS IT REALLY BEEN MORE THAN A YEAR? It has, Dave notes with amazement, actually been fourteen months since he moved here to the suburbs of New Jersey, about as far from the coolest place a single, unattached person could find himself. He is past thirty and no longer particularly confident—as he once was—that the future may hold the shimmering promise of something better for him. At least he's employed and can count on receiving, off the books, $350 in cash every Friday night, considerably more than he ever earned in the days when he and his band, The Dystopians, were in business together. If you could call it that. The gig he has now comes with free room and board, a plus, certainly, for someone earning the princely sum of $18,000 a year. The fact that Cheryl and Bill, his sister and brother-in-law, are his employers and that he inhabits a suite of rooms in their finished basement isn't information he likes to volunteer. But he will challenge anyone who might mock him to try living without that guarantee of money flowing in reliably from one week to the next. He and the other Dystopians had done that for years, sleeping in their van while on tour across the country, buying their clothes at a series of musty thrift shops, eating a couple of artery-clogging, fast-food meals a day, and all of it for *what*? For the sheer pleasure of creating and performing the kind of impressively fierce, energetic post-punk that somehow made Dave feel incandescent. Luminous. Transcendent. He hasn't felt that way in ages, and can't imagine the possibility of anything else making him feel that way ever again. He hasn't been in touch with his bandmates in a very long while. What would they think of him living in a McMansion in New Jersey, babysitting for the son of his sister's housekeeper every weekday from eight to four? *That is so fucked up, man,* he can hear them saying, and, on his worst days, he might not disagree too vehemently.

The child he takes care of is named Brady; at two and a half, despite Dave's best efforts, the kid still isn't toilet-trained. Maybe if his mother weren't so busy keeping house for Dave's sister, Brady might be out of diapers and into "big boy pants," as Dave calls them, trying, unsuccessfully, to render the words alluring. Brady has soaked through his overalls, Dave has just now discovered, and grabs the kid—all twenty-five pounds of him—and carries him, fireman-style, from the playroom into the bedroom here in the basement. Living upstairs in their own separate wing, Brady and his mother, Victoria, are half a floor above Dave's sister. They were already in place upstairs when Dave was offered his gig and basement suite; frankly, he's happy in the knowledge that Cheryl will never catch even the slightest trace of the weed he smokes every evening after the rest of the household is asleep. Cheryl and Bill are both nearing forty, and are litigation partners at a two hundred-lawyer firm in Manhattan. They have more money than any two people could possibly need, or so it seems to Dave, but Cheryl is on one of those SSRIs for depression, and despite looking thin and slight—scrawny, almost—she awakens at five every morning so she can work out on her treadmill for an hour before leaving for work. The brother-in-law (as Dave thinks of him) is bad news in a designer suit and a $300 silk tie, someone who berates waiters loudly and at length whenever his meals prove unsatisfactory in even the smallest way, and who often speaks to Cheryl as if she were a slow-witted child, despite her Phi Beta Kappa key and law degree from Georgetown. Smart enough for all that but dumb enough to have fallen for Bill—what's *that* all about? No wonder she's on Paxil or Zoloft or whatever it is she's taking—Dave can never remember which one, though he's seen the amber plastic pill bottle sitting next to the vitamins in one of the kitchen's numerous, gleaming glass-and-stainless-steel cabinets. It hurts him, knowing his sister is too disheartened to get through the day without it.

"So, little dude, what's with this diaper business?" Dave says now in his bedroom as he proceeds to get Brady out of his overalls and into a fresh diaper and a pair of flannel-lined jeans. It is mid-morning; upstairs, they can hear Victoria getting started on her vacuuming. "This is just plain stupid, man," Dave continues. "Every one of your buddies in the play group is, at the very least, wearing these"—he gestures toward a package of Huggies Pull-Ups training pants that he keeps around optimistically—"but you, you're just a big baby."

"Don't care," says Brady. "*Don't* care." Lying flat on his back, he smiles affably at Dave, who thinks, as he always does when he sees that jaunty smile, *damn cute*. He loves Brady's baby-soft, curly hair, his tiny, pure-white teeth, those pretty, hazel eyes inherited from his father, a Dominican guy Victoria hooked up with briefly a few years ago.

"Well, you *should* care," Dave says. "It's embarrassing, you know, when your little"—he almost says "peers"—"friends are way ahead of you. Especially since you're smarter than all of them put together. You're the one with the brains, dude."

Brady is clutching a Power Ranger figure in each hand,

one guy all in red with a silver weapon of some sort instead of a right arm, and one guy in a green outfit, with knee-high, gold-rimmed white boots. Brady brings the figures together, smashing their heads vigorously against one another, over and over again. "Brains, dude!" he says. "Ha ha ha."

"Stop smashing their heads together like that," Dave tells him. "How about you put them down and play with something else."

"Somethin' else," Brady agrees. Flipping over and slithering on his stomach down Dave's unmade bed, he flips again, and takes Dave's outstretched hand. They return to the playroom, a large, slightly drafty space softened with plush carpeting. Shoved against one wall are a plastic slide and a mini-trampoline. Along another stand a plastic sink overflowing with toy dishes; a beige plastic refrigerator/freezer stocked with toy food; a matching stove with several toy pots on its burners and a frying pan holding a single fried egg, its center a garish yellow, beside three strips of plastic bacon. All of which has been bought for Brady by Cheryl, who is convinced that without Victoria running the household, she, Cheryl, would be lost. Well, she can think whatever she likes, but Dave knows this is nuttiness. Or fuzzy thinking at best. On the other hand, without Victoria and Brady, he'd probably be temping at one or another of the many soulless corporations with offices in Manhattan, doing the sort of mind-deadening work he had his fill of in the years after The Dystopians broke up. Surprisingly, looking after Brady is far from the worst gig he's ever had. The kid is whip-smart and exuberant—excellent company most of the time—though occasionally he has furious tantrums that can persist for as long as an hour and from which he emerges sweaty and hoarse. When Brady is busy kicking and screaming over something as minor as a favorite sweatshirt languishing in the laundry hamper, Dave usually hooks himself up to his iPod and closes his eyes, opening them every couple of minutes to see if Brady is showing any signs of surrendering to good old common sense. Every job has its downside, Dave figures; dealing with a tantrum every few weeks beats endless hours of proofreading legal documents, doesn't it?

"What are you in the mood for, bro?" he asks Brady. "How about we check out the basket of toys." His voice lacks enthusiasm, he realizes, and to make up for it, he gives Brady a squeeze.

In the next moment Brady is ransacking the big wicker basket, tossing out a Jurassic Park III electronic dinosaur, a scowling, blond G.I. Joe, and Batman and Robin, both sporting special armor. Nothing suits Brady, apparently; he's walking away from the basket scornfully. "I'm bored," he announces.

"You don't even know what 'bored' means," Dave says. *And besides, it's only 10:30 in the morning, a long way from quittin' time.*

"Do *so*," says Brady.

"Oh yeah? Let's hear it."

"Well, it means the toys are stupid and I wanna go upstairs and see my mom."

"She's vacuuming," Dave says, "and she can't be disturbed. Not until four o'clock, when she's done working and we're done playing. Those are the house rules, bro. Etched in stone."

Brady engages now in some comically exaggerated eye-rolling, a display Dave has never been treated to before.

"Damn, you're funny!" he whoops. "We should get you an agent and put you in the movies." He finds himself fantasizing about a new career for both of them: Brady will be the next big child star in Hollywood and *he* will be his manager, in charge of safeguarding his millions, helping to groom his image, and, most important, negotiating and avoiding the pitfalls of fame for a toddler like Brady. (Dave is, in fact, familiar with a few of the perks of, if not exactly fame, then simply being a performer in the public arena, no matter how small: it's easy enough to vividly recall a handful of college girls clamoring for The Dystopians' autographs after a show, then inviting the band for some beers—and from time to time something a good deal more intimate—back in their dorm rooms. But this is ancient history and why bother to think about it now when all it does is underscore just what Dave has been missing.)

"*I'm* not funny," says Brady. "*You're* funny." He studies Dave briefly but intently, then concludes, "You're a silly billy!"

This is a compliment, Dave suspects, judging from the gleeful look on Brady's face. "Thanks," he says. "Not too many compliments coming my way this week or year, if you know what I mean."

Turning back to the basket of toys, Brady seizes a floppy-eared baby lion by its stuffed tail and swings it overhead like a lasso. "Bored bored bored," he pronounces.

"All right, I get the picture," Dave says. "Come on back to my room and we'll read some car magazines."

"Yasss!"

Squeezed into a leather lounger just big enough for the two of them, they spend the rest of the morning poring over *Car and Driver*, *Road and Track*, *Automobile*, and *Autoweek*, studying photographs of all the lustrous, brand new cars Dave covets and will never be able to afford, while Brady points with his small, stubby fingertip as he identifies, in his high-pitched little-boy voice, everything he sees. "Range Rover! Porsche! Mini Cooper! Honda! Lexus! BMW!" The kid can't read yet but he knows his cars and their emblems and never once makes a mistake, never once confuses a Ferrari with a Lamborghini or a Volvo with a Saab. One of these days Dave is going to take him to a car dealership and have him blow the salesmen right out of their seats. And this is what he's dreaming of now as his head tips forward and he dozes off, somewhere between breakfast and lunch, down here in the well-furnished basement of his sister's deluxe, super-sized McMansion.

He's wide awake, reading lamp blazing, when Cheryl decides to pay him a visit in his subterranean bedroom at 2:35 in the morning. He can't believe his crazy sister is dressed, in the middle of winter, in a one-piece, turquoise bathing suit, her hair concealed under a pale yellow shower cap, just so she can smoke one lousy, forbidden cigarette.

"You obviously don't understand," she tells Dave.

She's right, he doesn't. Doesn't understand how anyone could be so afraid of her husband finding out that she sneaks an occasional cigarette. "That's quite an outfit you're wearing," Dave says, trying not to stare too hard at her bony chest, her skinny, goose-bumped limbs, the hip bones that jut prominently from her bathing suit. Without those waves of her ginger-colored hair to soften it, her face looks angular, exposed, vulnerable. "I especially dig the shower cap," Dave jokes.

"If my hair smells like smoke, I'll never hear the end of it," Cheryl says as she gets comfortable in the leather chair she bought for him on a field trip they'd taken to Ikea when he'd first moved in. He'd been afraid to say how much he liked it, uneasy about letting her know just how grateful he was for the things she was bestowing upon him—a cozy chair, a suite of rooms, a weekly salary. There is, he thinks, something slightly creepy about being on the receiving end of all this from his sister; after all, he's thirty-two, an adult, surely. And then there's the brother-in-law, who clearly thinks him capable of very little and seems to take pleasure in letting Dave know it, making a big show of deliberately and unhurriedly extracting his credit card from his wallet whenever the three of them are out to dinner, never letting Dave pay the tab even when they're at an inexpensive place like the local diner, the brother-in-law saying, *Don't be ridiculous*, as Dave goes for his own wallet and a couple of twenties. The guy's easy-to-read message being, *I know it's too much for you to pay even for this, for these undistinguished hamburgers, this oily, grilled cheddar-and-bacon on whole-grain toast, that side order of overcooked onion rings.*

The price Dave pays, again and again, for having allowed his sister to rescue him.

"And in the old days," Cheryl is saying, "when I was at a pack a day, Bill used to say he could still smell the smoke even

155

after my clothing came back from the dry cleaners. Thus the bathing suit, which I'm going to hide in a little bag under the bathroom sink."

"I'd say Bill could use an attitude adjustment," Dave remarks, and drapes a plaid, satin-edged blanket around Cheryl's shoulders as she finishes up her cigarette. "You're freezing," he points out.

"That's all right, I'm going to take a nice hot shower in a few minutes. Gotta get the scent of smoke off my skin before I get back into bed."

"How about getting a divorce instead?" says Dave, absently thinking aloud.

"Hey!" Cheryl says. "I never said I didn't love him. Or that our marriage isn't a good, sound one."

"Sound," Dave repeats. "An odd word."

"I meant 'sound' as in 'stable.'"

"Right, and where's the romance in it?"

Cheryl yanks off her shower cap and squeezes it into a ball. "Where's the romance in *your* life, big shot?"

"Good one," says Dave. "You got me."

Fluffing out her hair now, looking more like her familiar self, Cheryl says, "You ever hear from Suzanne?"

"Suzanne who?" he says. He can be as cavalier as he likes, but, in truth, it pains him to conjure images of his ex and her sweetly open face, her child-sized fingernails and size 5 feet. "Oh, you mean that girl from Wisconsin?"

His sister throws the shower cap at him, but her aim is wild and the cap flies directly over his head, landing on the floor in a dark nest of yesterday's navy-blue boxers and gray socks.

"Well, thanks for stopping by," Dave says. "My door, as you know, is always open. And remember, *mi casa es su casa.*"

Cheryl rolls her eyes in that exaggerated way, just like Brady, and it occurs to Dave that this is where the kid must have seen it. Cheryl, he knows, has already started a college fund for Brady. And if Dave should ever want to return to school and pick up where he left off—in the middle of his junior year—she would be happy to finance that, too. He wishes he were ambitious enough to want to go back, wishes he could turn himself into that twenty-one-year-old so abundantly assured and confident. So expectant. To be honest, he can't imagine living with that kind of hopefulness ever again.

According to Suzanne, she had always known, with all certainty, that they were meant to spend their lives together. They even shared the same birthday, though Dave was a year older. The day he turned twenty-one, he announced his decision to drop out of Oberlin: over a birthday dinner two blocks from campus, in a substandard Japanese restaurant staffed by Mexican waiters, he told Suzanne that he was leaving school at the end of the semester, that his bandmates wanted to start touring and couldn't wait around for him to graduate. She might have said, as his parents did, later that week, *Are you out of your mind?* But instead she pushed aside her vegetable-and-tofu soup in its chipped ceramic cup and leaned across the Formica table to grab his elbows and say that she was coming with him. "I'll be your number one roadie," she said, "and you know, do the band's laundry and stuff like that." Dave was deeply gratified by her offer to cast her fate in with his, and he had to acknowledge that he'd savored, all semester, the pleasures of awakening to the lovely sight of her in his bed every morning. But by the time they were finished with their spicy yellowtail rolls and beef negimaki and the waiters had bid them *hasta luego*, he had just about persuaded her that being a roadie was no profession for someone as bright and capable as she was. Besides, there was no room for her in the van. And wouldn't it be helpful if one of them, at least, had a college degree? Suzanne had five semesters left, but a year and a half later, she graduated early and moved from Ohio to live with Dave in a tenement apartment on the Lower East Side of Manhattan, a gritty neighborhood where his great-grandparents had settled after arriving at Ellis Island at the beginning of the twentieth century. (This only added to his parents' distress and to their disappointment in him, and all Dave could do was shrug his shoulders, a gesture he found himself resorting to whenever he was trapped in that same tiresome conversation—the one that usually included the words "foolhardy" and "improvident"—with his mother and father.)

The tiny apartment on Eldridge Street had liver-colored linoleum floors that sloped, and was jammed with too many CDs and books; a collection of guitars was propped against the rarely dusted bookcase that swallowed up an entire wall. Several months after Suzanne moved in, Dave was stricken with appendicitis and suffered through an emergency appendectomy and five miserable days in Roosevelt Hospital. It was Suzanne who'd been smart enough to keep dragging him back to the emergency room, three days in a row, insisting to the ER docs—who kept sending him home without a diagnosis—that Dave was sicker than they thought. He owed his life to her, really, because when, at long last, an attending physician got the diagnosis right, Dave's appendix had nearly burst. In the evenings following his surgery, Suzanne slept in a chair at his bedside, going home to their apartment only to shower and change her clothes. She held miniature Dixie cups of water to his mouth, applied ointment to the cracked and bleeding corners of his lips, brushed his teeth for him, and, when he was able to get out of bed, walked him slowly and lovingly to the bathroom. (And if he'd needed help in there, she would have given it, he knew, never mind the embarrassment it might have caused them both.)

Now, years later, long after their relationship has come undone, he thinks of himself slumped in the emergency room the night of his surgery, watching while Suzanne, in her determined way, went after nurses and interns and attendings, standing her ground, arguing quietly and then fiercely, that her boyfriend needed their IMMEDIATE ATTENTION, GODDAMN IT! There had never been anyone so devoted to him, so unconditional in her love. Which was why it was impossible for him to fathom the news—when it was finally delivered—that he was no longer her boyfriend and had been displaced by someone named Ames. Who he'd logically though mistakenly assumed was a guy, but who was, as it turned out, nothing of the sort. Ames, he learned, had once been known as Amy, a name she found soft and saccharine, and she was a fifth-grade teacher in the public school where Suzanne taught in a special gifted and talented program. Their affair had begun while Dave and the band were off promoting their new CD on a month-long, cross-country tour, from which he'd phoned Suzanne, conscientiously and unfailingly, every single night.

"I go away for a big four weeks and what, suddenly you realize you're gay?" he'd said in disbelief. "Come on, this is a joke, right?" They had made love for what would be the very last time and were still in bed; Dave wiggled his toes, checking to see if he were actually awake, since what he'd just heard seemed to have sprung from a weird, unlikely nightmare.

"Of course I'm not gay," Suzanne said. "I assumed that would be more than a little obvious."

"So...what, then?" said Dave.

"Put it this way, don't you think sexuality is fluid?" Suzanne smiled at him patiently, as if he were one of her students, though perhaps not as gifted and talented as the rest.

"Fluid?" He thought immediately of semen and saliva and how often he'd marked her body with them. He'd never been greatly concerned with grammar, but he was well aware of the difference between a noun and an adjective, and knew he was on the wrong track here.

Suzanne sat up in bed, searched for her bra, and hooked it in place. "How about this: there are boundaries between gay and straight, right, and those boundaries are easily crossed. So yes, fluid."

There was no denying he considered himself pretty hip—he was a musician, a rock 'n' roller, and he'd done his share of exploring boundaries out there in the world—but he had no idea what the fuck Suzanne was talking about. "You're my girl-friend," he said helplessly. "We've been together for seven years. So don't tell me we don't love each other." He had to wait for her response, which wasn't forthcoming until the turtleneck of her sweater came down over her face and settled on her delicate collarbone.

"Dave, sweet pea," she said, and he must have been delud-ing himself, but even the way she uttered his name was like an embrace. "We *do* love each other, I think, but I have this thing with Ames, too, and right now it's just something I want to explore."

"Can't you explore this *thing*"—he struggled not to say the word angrily or contemptuously—"and stay here with me at the same time?"

The answer to this arrived without delay. "I'm afraid not, sweet pea. So what I need from you is to give me a little leeway here and we'll see how things go. And I want you to try and take it easy, okay?" She bent toward him and planted a kiss of tender apology on his cheek. "Now I'm going to get my stuff and get out of here, all right?"

It wasn't all right—it was utterly wrongheaded—but he couldn't figure out a way to stop her. His thoughts were scattered all over the place, his brain jumping from fluid to boundaries to Ames to dim, fuzzy images of Suzanne making love to a woman who couldn't be happy with the perfectly good name her parents had given her.

If tears had been permissible he might have shed them; instead, he made a visor of his hand and lowered his head, con-cealing his stricken face from Suzanne's shockingly, peculiarly unfamiliar one.

By the next day, his mind had cleared and he was able to see straight again, and he decided this bi-curiosity of hers was not unlike her yoga phase and her vegan phase, both of which had come and gone with a velocity he found amusing. So the plan was to wait patiently (or, more realistically, *impatiently*) until her interest in Ames diminished, as it inevitably would, and, in the interim, he and Suzanne would check in every couple of weeks, meeting for drinks, texting, talking on the phone, emailing each other. Allowing himself to believe it was just a temporary state of affairs, he managed to live this way for months, forcing himself to date a couple of women here and there while incurably in love with Suzanne. One night, at a time when their relationship had been reduced almost entirely to email, he saw that she had read and deleted his last two letters to her without responding. He discovered he just didn't have the heart to chase after her, surrendering instead to the realization that she and Ames had settled in for the long haul and weren't going to budge from their love nest in Park Slope. And yet, like someone who'd recently lost a lover under tragic circumstances, he still harbored hope that someday he would run into Suzanne and persuade her to return home with him.

Every once in a while on a Saturday, Victoria has something she needs to do for herself and doesn't want to take Brady along. Today, as he has in the past, Dave volunteers to watch him. Victoria is meeting a friend for lunch and a shopping expedition this afternoon, and after Dave gives her a lift into the city and drops her off at Macy's on 34th Street, he and Brady drive to Eleventh Avenue to check out the car dealerships that line both sides of the street. It is spring now, and in the fall Brady will start nursery school. What this will mean for Dave is unclear at the moment; certainly his time with Brady will be cut back and he'll have to look for a part-time job covering the fifteen hours a week that Brady will be attending the Toddle-In Preschool, next to a pizzeria in a small strip mall not far from Cheryl's home. Neither Cheryl nor Victoria has said a word to him yet on the subject, and whenever he allows himself to think about it, he feels both a sickening uneasiness and a vague melancholy:

Brady is growing up too fast. Dave can't imagine feeling any more nostalgic for Brady's rapidly disappearing childhood than he does, not even if he were Brady's father. Biological father? Adoptive father? He is, in fact, no father at all. He's the hired help, $350 a week plus room and board, and all-too-easily replaceable. You think he doesn't know that? And the craziest thing: fifteen years ago, when he was a high school senior, he was voted "Most Likely to Succeed." It was one of those small, Upper East Side private schools with an overabundance of bright, driven students, but the only thing *Dave* had been driven to wasn't even remotely connected to dazzling SAT scores or a stellar GPA. His band, the very first one he'd started, was called The Abyss, and their songs—every note and word of which had been written by Dave—must have touched a nerve. Because whenever they played, late at night in obscure clubs downtown in Alphabet City, their fellow students showed up, rocking to the belligerent, pissed-off, clamorous music that was Dave's gift to them. But it hits him now, in a realization that raises hackles all along the back of his neck, that perhaps the award for Most Likely to Succeed had been offered ironically; that really what was meant by the faux marble-and-gold trophy with his name printed in large block letters in Magic Marker was that he was the most unlikely of all to score big-time. If so, how prescient his classmates had been! What geniuses, to have accurately imagined his life in the twenty-first century, completely devoid of accomplishment, love, sex, and, of course, money.

"Let...me...out!" he hears a voice saying.

"What?" Dave says as he pulls up in front of a Mitsubishi dealership and puts the car in "park."

"Let me out, Dave!"

He turns around to see Brady tugging at the straps of his child-proof car seat. "Oh, sorry, dude." Stepping out of Cheryl's Mercedes, he frees Brady and helps him onto the sidewalk. "Hold my hand, okay?" Dave says, and Brady is already pulling him toward the entrance to the showroom. Inside, salesmen in sport coats and ties lounge at their desks, some fooling with their computers, others chatting on the phone and drinking coffee from mugs imprinted with the Mitsubishi logo. A handful of customers mill around, opening car doors and peering inside, running their hands across leather interiors and wondering aloud about sound systems and heated seats. Dave can't wait for Brady to shake a few of them up with what he himself can predict will be an astonishing performance.

Thirty-three inches tall, dressed in a sweatshirt emblazoned with a spike-tailed, blue-and-orange stegosaurus, Brady skitters across the showroom's glossy floor, singing out, "Eclipse! Lancer! Outlander! Galant!" his voice brimming with the confidence of one who knows his stuff and will not falter, that tiny, pudgy index finger of his—the one he'd learned to call "my pointer"—punctuating every word.

And here they come now, two middle-aged salesmen in mustard-yellow blazers sauntering over in tandem, followed by a third, this one clutching his coffee mug and spilling a little of it in his excitement, all three of them stupefied with amazement, awestruck, muttering *un-fucking-believable!* as Dave stands there in the middle of the showroom and beams, as proud as if he himself had given birth to Brady in the goddamn delivery room!

"More!" Brady cries, and, followed by Dave and the salesmen, he crosses the threshold into the adjacent dealership, where an assortment of Volkswagens awaits him. "Jettta!" Brady shouts. "Beetle! Golf! Passat!" he says, wrapping his mouth around the words, spitting out each of them joyfully.

"This kid just blows me away," a salesman says, shaking his head. Pinned to his forest-green sport coat is a badge revealing his name—G. Lucky Winslow. "He should be on TV or something."

"He's still in diapers," Dave brags. "He's just a baby, really."

"I'd put him in that whatchamacallit, *Believe It Or Not* book."

"*Ripley's*," says Dave.

"Right, and they've got a wax museum right here in the city, don't they? Just picture a wax figure of your little boy next to, like, Abraham Lincoln in that stovepipe hat, you know what I'm sayin'?"

"I believe that's Madame Tussauds," Dave says. But he decides not to correct Lucky's assumption about *your little boy*, because what's the harm, really? And in *this* city, anyway, it's not unlikely that a white guy with a dirty-blond beard might just be the father, or stepfather, of a darkly beautiful kid like Brady. And, too, shouldn't Dave be flattered by this case of mistaken identity? Who wouldn't be? Who wouldn't want to be linked to this diminutive car maven who studies *Autoweek* as if it were his own personal bible?

Lucky Winslow confers with his Mitsubishi colleagues and some Volkswagen salesmen, and they agree that Brady deserves a gift. En masse, they approach a locked glass case displaying a VW mousepad; billed black caps, their brims adorned with images of a GTI or The New Beetle; fancy, aluminum shift knobs; and a couple of model cars that can fit in your palm and happen to go for thirty-nine dollars a pop.

"You choose," Lucky Winslow instructs Brady. "You see anything you like there?"

"Beetle hat!" Brady says decisively, and someone goes off to find him a pipsqueak-sized one.

Eyeing the model cars, which, in his opinion, are the obvious—and smarter—choice, Dave rubs his knuckles lightly against the top of Brady's head.

"Carry me," Brady orders.

"Carry you where, buddy?"

"McDonald's."

"McDonald's is bad for you, as I believe I previously mentioned," Dave says, grimacing emphatically for Brady's benefit. "It'll make you fat and stupid, and we don't want that, do we?"

"McDonald's is *good* for me."

"Bad," Dave says. "Trust me on this." He looks around

impatiently for the guy who went to find the Beetle hat, but what he sees, instead, is a tanned, raven-haired, attractive woman in a tight-fitting T-shirt that brags, "NOBODY KNOWS I'M A LESBIAN!" Just what he's been looking for, a strikingly pretty woman who wants nothing to do with him. He turns back to Brady, who is still lobbying for McDonald's.

"Dave?"

"Yeah?" he says reflexively; it's a woman's voice and her hand is on his shoulder, and all at once he knows that he can't bear to turn around to look at her.

"Dave, it's me," the voice says. He has no choice but to acknowledge her and the hand that still rests on his shoulder.

"Hey you," he says. He is unprepared for the hug that comes next, for the scent of Suzanne's perfume or moisturizer or whatever it is he's forced to inhale that smells vaguely, tantalizingly, like caramel. As if diving underwater in his sister's backyard pool, he holds his breath for several moments and then has to come up for air. So Suzanne is a blonde now—one more shock for him to absorb—and she is, like her girlfriend in the boastful T-shirt, tanned as well. (A romantic vacation for two in Aruba? he speculates.) If only he felt nothing more than mild curiosity as he looks at her now. Or, even better, mild distaste.

No such luck.

But he is relieved, at least, to see that she's wearing some kind of leotard top and not that public announcement of a T-shirt like the woman he assumes is Ames, who is upon them now and offering her hand to Dave for a good, friendly shake.

"I'm Marissa," she says. "Nice to meet you."

"*Marissa?*" he says in confusion. For an instant, he feels a kinship with Ames, who he imagines was suddenly and unaccountably cast aside after years of steadfast love.

"So whatcha been doing for the past, what, three years?" Suzanne is saying.

"Oh, stuff…you know."

"The band still around?"

He tells her that The Dystopians dissolved shortly after the two of them had their own private breakup. "Our label sort of dropped us," he confesses, cutting to the chase. He shrugs, as if it were his parents he were speaking to and he were trying, yet again, to shield himself from their disappointment.

"Oh Dave," Suzanne says, "that's *horrible!*—this last word approaching, in that Midwestern accent of hers, something that might be spelled "whoor-able." And he can't help but feel a pang at the sound of that single ordinary word pronounced by her, as always, in that distinctive way.

"Dave, look!" Brady cries, and Dave realizes, guiltily, that he's forgotten all about the kid. "My Beetle hat!" One of the salesmen has arranged it on Brady, with the brim facing backward.

"Cool," Dave says. He scoops him up from the floor and Brady wraps his legs tight around Dave's waist.

"And who's *this* little cutie?" Suzanne says.

"This," Dave says, "is Brady." Suzanne and Marissa are staring quizzically, waiting for further information.

"Is he your son?" Suzanne mouths.

"It's complicated." That and a mysterious sigh are all he will allow himself to give her.

"I see," she says. But of course she doesn't and he wishes he could tell her that she couldn't possibly, not in a thousand years, fathom what is in that sigh. "Well, he's adorable in any case," Suzanne says. And to Brady, "Will you give me some sugar, honey? Right here," she says, pointing to her cheek. "One little kiss."

Bewitched, Brady obeys, and honors her with a small, shy kiss.

"Thank you, sir," Suzanne says, then nods when Marissa reminds her that they need to get busy on the paperwork for the car they've decided to lease.

"Which one?" Dave asks politely. He pretends to listen while Suzanne's girlfriend fills him in on their new Jetta, but all he can think of is finding his way to the nearest McDonald's.

With Victoria up front beside him and Brady asleep in the back, safely tethered to his seat, Dave cruises homeward through the Lincoln Tunnel and onto the Jersey Turnpike. The weekend traffic isn't nearly as heavy as he feared it would be, and his sister's almost-new Mercedes C280 drives like a fucking dream, and aren't these things to be grateful for?

Whoor-able, he hears himself say softly.

"Wanna see the jeans I found for Brady?" Victoria says. She is bent over and rummaging through the paper shopping bag at her feet. "So cute, and on sale for $10.99, right?"

Whoor-able, he murmurs, caressing the word, as though it were something Suzanne had—in an impulsive burst of generosity and affection—bestowed on him today, a small but priceless keepsake that's his to hang onto for as long as he desires.

THE SNACK BAR AT AUSCHWITZ

⋮

AT THE BUS STOP AT MATEJKO SQUARE in Krakow, Nathaniel and his fiancée stand on the sidewalk behind a metal sign that resembles, in size and shape, one that in their native Manhattan might read "NO PARKING TUES THURS 9 A.M. 10 A.M." This sign, however, announces eagerly in English:

TRIP TO AUSCHWITZ-BIRKENAU
SALT MINES
AND MORE!

It is one of those particularly pleasing days in April, ideal for sightseeing—either the most notorious of concentration camps or the salt mines, your choice. The sun is high and exceptionally bright, the temperature a warmish sixty degrees; all you really need for outerwear is a light jacket or sweatshirt. There are a couple of dozen tourists waiting along with Nathaniel and Julia for the bus, all of them chatting in German or Polish, lots of flaxen hair gleaming in the sunlight. Not one among them is Jewish, Nathaniel would bet his life on it. And this is a good thing, he thinks—hey, isn't it the gentiles who need to see precisely what happened to European Jewry in the darkest years of the twentieth century? The Jews themselves presumably know all about it, know that though there were more than three million Jews in pre-war Poland, the population today is a meager twenty-five thousand or so.

Julia, raised Catholic, had always heard, she told Nathaniel earnestly when they first met, that Jewish men make the best husbands. That remains to be seen—their wedding date is four months off, at the end of the summer, and who knows what sins, venial or mortal, Nathaniel may be guilty of in the future. He's been on his best behavior during this trip of theirs, the one Julia jokingly refers to as "Nathaniel's Depressing Holocaust Tour." Before arriving in Krakow, they'd been in Prague, where they visited Kafka's grave and learned that his three sisters had been killed in the Holocaust. ("Pretty freakin' depressing, don't you think," Julia had muttered under her breath. She's an oncology nurse and knows all about depressing, as does Nathaniel, a psychologist specializing in eating disorders.) They'd taken a walking tour in Prague of the Old Jewish Quarter, a place, their guide promised, where "the tragic destiny of the Jews becomes alive again." ("Oh boy, here we go," Julia said, hearing this, and sighed loudly). Crossing the Charles Bridge by foot to the Lesser Town Square, where they rode the tram to the Prague Castle, Julia seemed to perk up considerably. Not a word was mentioned in the castle about the Jews and the bitter truth of their history in Prague.

The Auschwitz-Birkenau bus arrives right on schedule and a small, smiling woman in her twenties steps out to greet her customers. She's sporting a brown shirtwaist dress with a green kerchief tied at her neck; on her feet are anklets and sensible brown shoes. She reminds Nathaniel of the little girls in his class in fourth grade dressed in their Brownie uniforms. Her name is Elzbieta, she says in lightly accented English, and explains that although she is fluent in German, and, of course, Polish, this is an English-speaking tour. She explains, too, that while they are en route to their destination—"the best known place of genocide in the world," she says, sounding oddly and mystifyingly enthusiastic, a saleswoman hawking her wares with pride—they will be watching documentary footage shot by a Russian cameraman who was present at the liberation of the camp in 1945. "You will see some very disturbing things," she promises, and shrugs.

The group settles quietly into their comfortable, well-cushioned seats. The film begins immediately; its narration is in Russian, with Polish, German, and English subtitles, take your pick. "Time has no power over these memories," the first subtitle reads. On the screen behind the bus driver are black-and-white images of trenches lined with skeletal corpses—hundreds, thousands, tens of thousands, who can keep score? Emaciated children in striped uniforms pull up their shirt sleeves obligingly to show the tattooed numbers embellishing their heartbreaking, bone-thin arms.

"I kinda hate movies with subtitles," Julia confesses, her voice tinged with apology, and she rests her head on Nathaniel's shoulder. Her eyes close; he lets her sleep, his hand occasionally reaching out to fondle her longish, pale hair until, ninety minutes later, the bus pulls into the Auschwitz parking lot.

"Auschwitz" and "parking lot"—the proximity of these words seems slightly preposterous, and Nathaniel imagines a member of the SS driving home from work during rush hour in 1944, met at the front door by his devoted wife at the end of the day.

Hard day at the office, Klaus?

And he, Nathaniel, already in a leaden mood, ain't seen nothin' yet.

"Now I will say to you goodbye." Elzbieta smiles, delivering the group into the hands of an official Auschwitz guide named Katarzyna, a bosomy, middle-aged woman in those same sensible shoes. Unlike Elzbieta, however, Katarzyna looks none too happy to be at work today.

"We will see each other again after your tour is over. We hope you will enjoy the many interesting things there are to see here," Elzbieta says, still smiling sweetly.

Interesting things?

You betcha.

Katarzyna begins her speech, telling Nathaniel and Julia and their group of twenty-five or so, as soon as they pass through the *Arbeit Macht Frei* gate, that 960,000 Jews died at Auschwitz. And let's not forget, she says, the Romany, the homosexuals, the Soviet POWs, the Polish political prisoners. But primarily Jews, Jews, and more Jews. Among them Nathaniel's grandfather's twin sisters, Hannah and Anne-Sophie, who were arrested in their home in Vienna, along with Nathaniel's grandfather, and were twelve at the time of their deaths.

"Their ashes were used as fertilizer," Katarzyna says wearily, though, for the most part, her voice is without affect. As she speaks, Japanese sightseers cruise by with their babies in Snugglies. A sweetly pretty nun in full black-and-white habit, her fluorescent green backpack a lively splash of color, strolls past. Polish tourists chauffeur toddlers in strollers; iPhones in hand, the Poles text madly. To whom? And why?

And why, in God's name, would you bring your babies and two-year-olds here? Here is where, toward the end of the war, in an effort to save money on gas, Katarzyna reports, Jewish children (possibly Hannah and Anne-Sophie, Nathaniel speculates, his stomach churning) were tossed alive into the ovens and into open, burning pits. And, by the way, this is also the place where Dr. Herta Oberhauser, a female physician, liked to rub ground glass and sawdust into the wounds of young children. Just for the hell of it? For her own personal pleasure? Katarzyna doesn't know. She knows, however, that after the war, appropriately enough, Dr. Oberhauser became a family practitioner in Germany.

There's no denying the loveliness of this spring day; birds warble in their high-pitched voices in the sunlight over Auschwitz now. Searching for his sunglasses in his messenger bag, Nathaniel slips them on; his brimming eyes are nobody's damn business. Julia grasps his hand and squeezes it a little too hard.

Katarzyna escorts them to Block 15, a brick barracks where they will see images familiar to anyone at all who has ever made the effort to flip through certain books, view certain documentaries, or click onto certain Internet sites. But standing here like this, silent and motionless as wax figures as they take in the sight of enormous glass cases full of human hair cut from murdered prisoners, well, this, baby, is what's known as up close and personal, Nathaniel thinks.

This human hair, shorn seven decades ago, is mostly gray, but you can't miss that pair of blondish pigtails and a single, auburn ponytail clipped from the heads of two little girls (possibly named Hannah or Anne-Sophie) after their trip to the gas chamber. Nathaniel Schonfeld, twenty-nine years old, six feet two inches tall, a solid, healthy, one hundred and sixty-five pounds or so, has a good strong stomach, but today—as Katarzyna discloses that the hair of these victims was used to manufacture felt and thread by the German textile industry—he feels distinctly queasy. Nauseated.

"Yuck," he hears Julia murmur. Or maybe it's "yikes."

There are other rooms, other floor-to-ceiling glass cases, some displaying a tangle of thousands of wire-rimmed eye glasses and old-fashioned monocles; another densely packed with toothbrushes and hairbrushes, one hairbrush a startling sky-blue among the countless drab ones. And another glass case loaded with baby shoes and children's shoes, a pitiful mountain of stolen maryjanes and oxfords and ankle-high booties rising all the way to the ceiling. Nathaniel knows that what he's thinking—that each toothbrush, each hairbrush, each pair of gaily decorated little-girl shoes represents a single, idiosyncratic human life so cruelly cut short by monstrous fiat of a lunatic—well, let's face it, even if one or two or twelve of those innocent snuffed-out lives belonged to someone in *his* own family, *even then* what he's thinking is still entirely, pathetically, unoriginal.

It ain't much, but it's all he's got, and it's heartfelt.

Out in the hallway, as Katarzyna's group moves along from one room to the next with other, similarly silent and shell-shocked groups of tourists from all over the world, Nathaniel notices a steely, straight-backed woman who'd been seated across the aisle from him on the bus. Fiftyish, dressed in hiking shorts, work boots, and woolen sweat socks, the woman collapses without warning against the hallway's brick wall, sobbing wildly, barely able to catch her breath as she weeps, "I, I, I...I can't..." She's German—Nathaniel heard her speaking on the bus—but she's crying out in English as Katarzyna squats on the floor next to her, trying to offer some solace. Though Nathaniel will never admit it, the exquisite satisfaction he feels at the sight of this German wracked with sorrow is, he realizes now, what he's always wanted—to hear even a single German weep like this, if only for a moment or two, here in the barracks of "the best known place of genocide in the world."

———

Last summer, Julia was on her way out of Gourmet Garage clutching a plastic bag of rock-hard peaches and half a pound of prosciutto, sliced extra-thin, when one of the printed notices push-pinned into the cork board near the store's exit happened to catch her eye:

ARE YOU IN LOVE?
HAVE YOU BEEN IN YOUR CURRENT
RELATIONSHIP FOR LESS THAN A YEAR?

Well, yes. And yes.

Whoever tacked up the notice had been looking for volunteers between the ages of eighteen and thirty-nine to participate in a study of ROMANTIC LOVE—the two words set apart from the rest in an extra-large font, as if whoever had typed them had been shouting out loud. This person, pwang@ ccny.cuny.edu, was extending an invitation to Julia and her partner (a word Julia always imagined in ironic quotation marks) to talk about their experiences. Mr./Ms. Wang had not, however, specified where or when: Julia would have to email him or her for further details. Rarely one to turn down an invitation, she thought she just might accept this one. Though without Nathaniel, of course, she wouldn't be welcome, and who knew if he'd be willing?

They had just moved in together, having left Manhattan to rent a strange little two-story carriage house in Brooklyn in a neighborhood full of twenty-something hipsters. Their neighbors across the courtyard, Bonnie and Phil, were a couple of drug-dealing stoners, Julia was sure of it; they both looked wasted nearly every time she saw them. Sometimes she heard them shrieking obscenities at each other late at night from their terrace. When Julia occasionally saw Bonnie on her way to the subway in the morning, Bonnie, pallid and sleepy-looking, always pretended she didn't know her. And one morning she appeared with a poorly concealed black eye, the sight of which compelled Julia to take her business card from her wallet and offer it to her.

"Lenox Hill Hospital—wait, you think I'm sick or something?" Bonnie said scornfully. "Could you please please *please* mind your own fucking business?"

"If you need any help…" Julia said, because how could you turn away silently from that bruised eye of hers?

Well, maybe some people could, but *she* couldn't.

Nathaniel, it turned out, wasn't interested in participating in the study of romantic love. "What are we, cast members of some stupid reality show dying to blab about our personal lives?" he said when she asked him.

"I just thought it might have been fun, that's all," Julia told Nathaniel, who, she'd thought, would have understood that she, of all people, could use a little fun in her life. That night, she'd arrived home from work feeling completely drained. She and Caroline, a fellow oncology nurse, had planned a senior prom of sorts for an eighteen-year-old patient who had, they knew, only the slimmest chance of surviving past the summer, never mind his nineteenth birthday. They invited his girlfriend and several dozen of his high school pals, all of whom dressed for the occasion; they even persuaded a couple of his doctors to show up in tuxedos in the hospital cafeteria, where Julia and Caroline had installed a CD player and speakers and whose ceiling they'd decorated with silvery balloons. That poor eighteen-year-old, Patrick Tarasiewicz, had no future, but at least he had this, Julia told herself. And then, at home after the ersatz prom, she talked Nathaniel into making her a trio of margaritas, just to take the edge off. He even ran out to the liquor store to get her the tequila, and to the Korean grocer for fresh limes. Afterward, when she was too drunk to make it safely from the living room to their bedroom, which required a short trip down a flight of stairs with no railing, Nathaniel gathered her up from the couch, and carried her to their bed. Lovingly and uncomplainingly. When she awoke the next morning with a killer hangover, he brought Alka-Seltzer and a tall glass of water to her bedside but didn't deliver, as he might have, one of those I-told-you-three-was-too-much lectures.

He might not have wanted to volunteer for the romantic love study thing, but he was good husband material, of that there was no doubt.

In Hungary, Katarzyna informs them, all telephone service to Jewish customers was shut off in 1944; they were forbidden, as well, to use public phones. Before being transported to Auschwitz to be slaughtered, the Hungarian Jews were locked into pigsties.

"Guess they would have taken away their iPhones, too," Nathaniel hears a girlish voice behind him say.

"And their BlackBerries," someone else adds.

"Heinrich Himmler, the SS Reichsführer, made a speech about the Jews on October six, nineteen forty-three," Katarzyna begins. She wrings her hands. "This is what he said: 'The difficult decision had to be taken to make this people disappear from the earth.'"

"And their BlackBerries, don't you think?" that same voice behind Nathaniel insists.

In a room full of black-and-white photographs snapped by Nazis proud to document their glorious achievements, Nathaniel is mesmerized by a picture of a barefoot man who looks to be no older than Nathaniel himself, and who is cradling a small child against him; the photo has caught them in midair, at the very last moments of their lives as they leap into the pit where they will land DOA—an instant after the SS, machine guns poised, will shoot them down. As if they were nothing more than a couple of birds flying overhead, perfect for target practice.

The weepy German tourist is nowhere to be found; later, Nathaniel and Julia will see her in the snack bar, sipping an espresso contemplatively, pinky curved and raised in the air, her tears dried.

Nathaniel corners Katarzyna just after she instructs the group to give themselves a half-hour break. He asks, with genuine curiosity, what it's like for her to do her work here, unflinchingly, day after day repeating the ghastly statistics, the gruesome, repellent details, to one group of tourists after another. He asks, warily, if the words she utters have become, over time and in the endless repetition, meaningless to her. And then asks her forgiveness for having broached the subject at all.

"No, no," she says, waving away his apologies. Her face is broad and very white, her mouth a little pinched, her eyes a rinsed blue; there's a simple crucifix around her neck and an unadorned gold band on the middle finger of her left hand. Her nails are blunt and unpolished. The words she's memorized still have the power to raise goose bumps at the back of her neck, she says. "But at five o'clock, when it is time for me to go home to my husband and my son, I do not think of any of this. Because if I did, I would just want to die, if you understand."

Yes, Nathaniel says, he absolutely understands. He's relieved to hear that there's a husband and son; he would hate the thought of her returning to an empty house, an empty life, after a day spent leading tours through this wretched place.

Beside him, Julia leans forward and pats Katarzyna's arm. "Thank you," Julia says.

The offerings at the Auschwitz snack bar are nothing to write home about, they discover. But they'll suffice, for those hardy souls who still have an appetite after a peek inside the one remaining gas chamber the Nazis left behind here. And here's what your *zlotys* can buy if you're starving or just vaguely hungry: "sour rye soup, sausage stew, hot dog, pizza, Lipton tea." There's an additional charge for sugar cubes, mustard, and ketchup.

"You're not angry at me, are you?" Julia asks as they settle at a table for two.

"What?" Nathaniel says. He sips at his Styrofoam cup of tea, which has a funny taste and smell, a little gamy, he thinks, though maybe it's just his imagination.

"You seem a little, I don't know, distant?" Frowning at him, Julia says, "I can't *believe* you had to pay for the sugar in your tea. And charging extra for ketchup? I mean, come *on*, that is *so* fucked up." Taking the first small bite out of her slice of pizza, she announces, "This is THE worst pizza I've ever had in my life. It's a disgrace. I mean, they should be ashamed of themselves," she says, indignant.

They *should* be ashamed of themselves, and the pizza's the least of it, Nathaniel starts to say, then decides to keep it to himself.

"The crust is tasteless, and too thick, plus the cheese is too salty…" Julia takes another, bigger, more adventuresome bite. "Like it would kill them to use fresh mozzarella and basil," she says bitterly.

"You think you're at Lombardi's on Spring Street—this is Auschwitz!" Nathaniel says, raising his voice a little too loud. At adjacent tables, Poles and Germans and Hungarians are turning to stare at him. He wonders if they know he's a Jew, engaged to be married to someone who has nothing much to say about Nazi atrocities but finds it easy to get all worked up over the inferior pizza served at the snack bar. He looks at Julia, who is gazing up at the menu board, searching for something better for herself. Absently, he starts to whistle. This is how he and Julia first met, Nathaniel whistling on the subway platform at Times Square, attracting Julia's attention with his rendering of "Younger Than Springtime" while the two of them, strangers who happened to be waiting for the shuttle that would take them to Grand Central, stood side by side. He'd just gone to the theatre with his mother and stepfather, who'd insisted he see *South Pacific* with them, knowing full well that Nathaniel, a big Dylan and Neil Young fan with 9,000 songs on his iPod (mostly rock, but including a smattering of blues and jazz), had a strong dislike for musical theatre, whose narratives he generally found just plain mindless, and whose music he thought saccharine.

"I *know* that song!" Julia had said to him, smiling. "*Softer than starlight are yewww,*" she sang in a pretty good soprano, and even then he hadn't realized, until Julia pointed it out to him, that the song he'd been whistling was "Younger Than Springtime."

"From *South Pacific*, right?" she said. Though it was winter, she was wearing a thin, summery dress with leggings, a hooded sweatshirt, and plaid canvas sneakers. A second sweatshirt was wrapped around her small waist. Her dark eyes were lined on the bottom in black, and her hair was so flawlessly straight that Nathaniel suspected she must have used one of those expensive irons his ex-girlfriend was so fond of. She looked a little waifish, a little lost, which he found terrifically appealing.

"I hate show music," he confessed, embarrassed to have been caught whistling a Rodgers and Hammerstein classic. But Julia didn't hold it against him.

"I totally get it—you were whistling 'Younger Than Springtime' because you hate it," she said, and smiled at him again. "No problem."

She'd recently broken up with a long-term boyfriend, a radiology resident at Lenox Hill, she told Nathaniel a few nights later when they met, as planned, at a Starbucks on the Upper West Side, close to where she was living with two friends from college. She confided that she loved her job working with critically ill children and teenagers, though it wore her out, and that sometimes, when her shift was over, she took a cab home through the Park, closed the door of her bedroom so her roommates wouldn't hear her, and cried for a while until she felt better. Not very professional of her, she said, but there you have it. Julia listened sympathetically to Nathaniel's stories about his clients, mostly teenage girls who were addicted to their bingeing and purging and were unable to explain to their overwrought parents just why it was that they couldn't stop. The girls sometimes signed waivers allowing Nathaniel to speak to their parents, who called him on his cell phone, begging for an update, for a morsel of good news.

He thought of his clients, their slender index fingers compulsively thrust down their throats, acid from their bile eating away at the enamel of their pearly whites and their dentists asking if they were in the habit of sucking lemons because how else to explain those ruined teeth of theirs? All of it seemed sort of inconsequential once he heard the stories of Julia's patients and their battles just to stay alive from one day to the next. And after a while he saw that he'd fallen in love with her goodness, with her willingness to devote herself, without complaint, to the sickest and most vulnerable of people.

But now he recognizes her for what she evidently is—someone who finds fault with the pizza at Auschwitz and just won't shut up about it.

"I wanna go home," she tells him, and at first he thinks she means their perfectly nice hotel in Krakow. But what she really means is back to their weird little carriage house with the shiny granite floors and cheap linoleum countertops and their bedroom that affords them a clear view of their crazy neighbors blissfully smoking crack (*she* thinks it's only pot, but *he* knows better) on the terrace across the shared courtyard.

"But what about Budapest?" he says, because that's their next stop and last leg of their trip.

She doesn't wanna go to Budapest, she says, and she's sick of the crappy food and the sad, sad stories everywhere they've been and all the plaques on walls and doors and iron gates in memory of those *whose blood was spilled like water by the Nazi beasts or whatever.*

He's stung, and feels like shaking her, but he can already imagine the crimson print of his hands marking her sweet white shoulders and it's too much for him.

Taking one more sip of his toxic tea, he leads Julia out to the parking lot, but fails to convince her to join him on the tour bus for the short ride to Birkenau two miles away. Where, like countless tourists before him, he will drop to his knees and collect a handful of rocks from along the railroad tracks that once lined the way from all over Eastern Europe to the killing fields of Birkenau—and bring those small gray rocks home with him to Williamsburg, Brooklyn, gently wrapped in clean white tissues.

In Brooklyn he will wash the rocks with liquid soap and a fine spray of warm water. And, ignoring Julia's protests, arrange each of them delicately on their cluttered bookcase, where he will return, anytime he wants, just to feel their weight in his palm.

KOSTA

O F THE OLD DAYS, Kosta remembered absolutely nothing, and why would he? He was, he explained to Rachel, a mere infant at the time his parents had been wrenched away from him in the middle of the night and then, horrifyingly, executed only hours later. Shot to death by Stalin's thugs in a prison courtyard in Leningrad. For no good reason at all except that they were a couple of Jewish doctors—his mother an obstetrician, his father a surgeon—two well-educated professionals whom the madman Stalin feared and hated, though of course he'd never even laid eyes upon them. "Nice, huh?" Kosta said.

"Jesus Christ!" said Rachel, and impulsively placed a hand on Kosta's well-haired wrist. She and Kosta had never spoken in person before, and while at first she didn't find herself particularly attracted to him—despite his big, florid, handsome face—she did have the momentary urge to embrace his bulky shoulders, to bend his head benevolently against her and say something soothing. Something akin to "there, there," a phrase she couldn't recall ever having heard in real life but which seemed appropriate under the circumstances. Instead, she shook her head gloomily and sipped her white chocolate latte in its environmentally friendly paper cup.

Rachel was an unemployed, never-married thirty-year-old, and Kosta, a successful businessman, was a divorced fifty-something; they had not a thing in common, really. He was, however, going to pay her a generous sum of money ($45,000, to be exact) to write the story of his life, a story he was convinced could be sold to a publisher and then to the movies if Rachel did her job right. And so they were sitting together now in a Starbucks in Union Square, with their absurdly expensive coffees and a single, untouched, caramel praline muffin on a brown paper napkin between them. It was nearly four o'clock on a drizzly Sunday in late November, and the place was packed with holiday shoppers, all of whom seemed to have cell phones set out on their tables, waiting, perhaps, for an urgent call from the love of their lives. Though Rachel was currently without a lover, she did have a cell phone, a bachelor's degree from Brown (where she'd been a comp lit major), a master's from Columbia, and a bad habit of falling for men for whom long-term commitment remained an unappealing concept. Having recently walked away from an unsatisfying job as a book publicist, she had been only too happy to read Kosta's email response to the ad she'd placed in the *Times Book Review*—one that announced her services as a "ghost writer par excellence." She had yet to ghost-write anything, in fact, but she'd accumulated plenty of A's on her papers at both Brown and Columbia, labored over countless press releases, and, on her good days, had enough self-confidence to keep her going. Earlier in the week, over the phone, she took a deep breath and tried not to sound anxious as she assured Kosta of her many virtues, including meticulousness and punctuality, and after a brief pause, he'd replied, "Okay, sounds cool."

Here in Starbucks, he pinched off a surprisingly dainty piece from their muffin, and, with his other hand, flicked back his thick, dark ponytail, which reached just past his shoulders. "Not only that," he said, "but after my parents were murdered, my own relatives fucking disavowed me!" Over fifty years had passed since he'd been abandoned, but he seemed newly outraged, as if the cruel facts of his autobiography still pained him. "Those relatives in Leningrad thought it was too dangerous to take me in, so they dumped me at some adoption agency, and eventually I ended up in Jersey City, in the home of two lunatics named Dorothy and Bobby Morrison, adoptive parents who treated me like their own personal servant boy, and beat the crap out of me if I didn't clean up my room properly."

Rachel wiped away a tear. She couldn't bear to look at Kosta; she had to look somewhere, anywhere, else. To her left, a trio of homeless guys, their heads bowed, ignored a fat, battered paperback entitled *Embracing Defeat*, which someone had apparently left behind on their table.

"It was a long time ago, but you can see I've still got anger issues," Kosta said. He offered the muffin to her, reaching over and holding it up to her mouth. "Don't you want some?"

"Just thinking about what happened to your parents—what happened to *you*—makes my stomach hurt," said Rachel.

"Well, I envy you those loving parents you probably have."

"I do have them, actually. Very much so," Rachel admitted. She almost felt as if she owed him an apology for her untroubled, uneventful childhood and adolescence, for the openly affectionate parents, who, to this day, regarded her and her older brother, Ezra, as the shining jewels that ornamented their long and generally happy marriage.

"Well, then, you hit the jackpot, babe! You won the lottery ten times over! Two loving parents and you're good to go. Two lousy adoptive parents and you're permanently fucked."

Under her breath, Rachel cursed the execrable Dorothy and Bobby Morrison, they who had treated Kosta so shamefully, bloodying his nose, he told her, sending him to school now and again with a blackened eye, a shiner that would eventually turn shades of green and yellow before fading away completely. But these were details Rachel wouldn't learn until a month later, the night when she and Kosta stripped down to their underwear and fell across his unmade bed together, their hearts thumping in perfect synch with one another, their breathing noisy and a little ragged.

Christmas Eve, Kosta grilled a dinner for the two of them on the roof of the building he lived in near NYU. On the grill next to the steaks were half a pound of shiitake mushrooms that had been marinated for an hour in a vinaigrette of his own invention. There was no salad, but there were glass bowls of artichoke hearts and baby carrots, and a hard Italian bread called a *stirato*, pieces of which he warmed in a toaster oven whose innards, Rachel noticed, could have used a good cleaning. She had never been to his apartment before, though they had worked together three weekends in a row at her dining table in a walk-up on the Upper East Side. She had several dozen pages of notes transcribed from the oral history Kosta had spilled to her thus far; she wasn't sure, however, precisely where the project was headed. Most of what Kosta had told her involved his miserable upbringing in Jersey City, and the hatred he felt for those unseemly parents who just wouldn't give him a break but who showered upon their own two biological sons an extravagant love which, Kosta claimed, made him want to puke whenever he thought about it.

From the roof, Rachel could see the Empire State Building in the near distance, its upper floors lit in a slightly fuzzy red and green in honor of the holiday season. She shivered in her down vest, and rubbed her mittened hands together as Kosta, in his shirtsleeves, tended to their main course, three generous-sized porterhouse steaks that he'd bought from a pricey butcher in SoHo. There was a table of metal and frosted glass with three wrought iron chairs arranged around it, and it was here that Kosta hoped they would enjoy their dinner. But the temperature was below forty, Rachel was sure of it, and a sudden icy breeze lifted the royal blue napkins he had instructed her to place on the table after she'd Windexed it with a couple of flimsy paper towels a few minutes earlier.

She came up behind him at the grill and touched his elbow. "We're going to have to eat indoors," she said. "I'm sorry, but I'm just too cold."

"What? Really?" He turned toward her, his face rosier than usual in the light of the fire. "Are you sure?"

Nodding, she said, "I'm going inside now. To the bathroom. And then I'll be back, okay?"

"Here's the thing," Kosta said, brandishing a long knife with a six-inch blade that dripped blood from the porterhouse he'd slit open. "The bathroom's down the hall."

"Down the hall from the living room? I'll find it."

"No no," he said, and gave her a smile tinged with discomfort. "I mean down the hall from the *apartment*."

Rachel knew it was a commercial building, with only the top three floors rented out to residential tenants, but, even so, what was he talking about? "Everyone on your floor uses the same bathroom?" she said, shocked.

For the first time since they'd known each other, he put his arm around her; in his other hand, he still held the knife. "It's just me," he said. "All the other apartments have their own bathrooms. But what I've got is even better, a whole men's room to myself. No one ever uses it except me. It's got three stalls and three sinks, and I pay good money to one of the cleaning ladies who works for the building's management to keep it pristine." The only problem, he continued, was that he had to take the elevator down a dozen flights to use the shower in the ladies' room on the fourth floor. Before seven a.m., and after nine p.m., when all the commercial tenants were gone.

"No way!" Rachel said, and imagined Kosta striding along the cold, uncarpeted corridor and into the elevator, dressed in a bathrobe and flip-flops, loaded down with bottles of shampoo and conditioner, and a bar of soap in a covered plastic dish.

"Do you think any less of me because I have to shower in the ladies' room?" Kosta asked. "Listen, the software company I own is worth a couple of million—I could sell it tomorrow if I wanted to. You know, cash it all in and move to the Bahamas or something. My point being that I could move out of here any-time I like, but I choose not to."

"Why would I think any less of you?" Rachel said. Still shivering, she snuggled into his embrace. What she *did* think was that this weird shower-and-bathroom situation was the leg-acy of his wretched early years, and that it could be traced all the way back to the execution of his parents by henchmen in cahoots with a murderous psychopath.

"But do I need a key to get into the bathroom?" she asked.

"No key. And it's totally safe, I promise."

"Fine, but can I bring you back a jacket? Aren't you cold?"

"Got my fat to keep me warm," Kosta said, pinching together some flesh at his ribs.

"Yeah, right, you're real fat," Rachel teased. "Though, actu-ally, you *are* a big tall guy."

"Always one of the guys in the back row in every class picture, year after year. The one with his head sticking up above everyone else's. Even in kindergarten." The steaks hissed on the grill; behind the high windows of an apartment in an adjacent building, a man stood playing a violin. "I wonder if my father was a big guy as well," Kosta mused.

Of course Kosta had no photographs of him, Rachel real-ized. Or of his mother. This seemed pitiful, to have been denied even a snapshot or two. She tilted her face upward and kissed his lips—what else did she have to give him?

His mouth opened and he returned her kiss. It was dark on the roof except for the full moon and the lighted windows of the buildings all around them. It had been months since she'd kissed a man; the last time was during the summer, on the ferry back from Fire Island, when she and Henry, her boyfriend of almost a year, were deciding whether or not to break up. By the time the ferry docked in Bay Shore, Henry confessed that the thought of marriage had never crossed his mind and that the fact that Rachel's thirtieth birthday had recently come and gone was no incentive whatsoever to pop the question. They rode the train back to the city in silence, and just before arriving at Penn Station, Rachel told him, in a tiny voice, that the year they'd spent together was long enough. *Long enough for what?* Henry wanted to know, but there seemed no point in responding to his clueless question.

She pulled gently away from Kosta now so she could study his face. It wasn't the face of an older man; it was unlined, and his neatly groomed beard and moustache, along with his ponytail, were still mostly black. He was only a few years younger than her father, who looked so much older. She wondered what her parents would think if they knew about the kiss she'd shared with Kosta. Rachel would always be their child; they still referred to her and her brother as "the kids" when they talked about them. "It's such a pleasure to have the kids around," she'd heard her mother tell her father at Thanksgiving, as if she and Ezra were kindergartners and the four of them still lived under the same roof. But she wanted, at that moment, for Kosta to meet her parents, to see what it was like to be enfolded by a loving family, particularly a mother upon whose shoulders you could weep after your boyfriend in grad school revealed that the word "fiancée" gave him the chills—and not the good kind, either.

Kosta wasn't exaggerating, Rachel discovered as she entered the men's room; the place was immaculate. She couldn't bring herself to sit down on the toilet when she peed, but that was *her* problem, and no fault of the cleaning woman who'd shined up the three black sinks and the pink-and-black granite countertop that surrounded them. The floor, of veined marble, was improbably pristine, the mirror that stretched across the length of the sinks was smudgeless, and the liquid soap she used on her hands was dispensed from a vase-like silver bottle and smelled faintly of honeydew. It was the one and only men's room she'd ever visited and she had no complaints. Even so, wasn't there something just the slightest bit disconcerting about a guy with his very own men's room? Perhaps, if she were to tell her friends about him, she would simply describe him as eccentric.

They ate their dinner in the living room, and Kosta polished off a bottle of merlot with a little help from Rachel. Afterward, they settled into a worn leather couch, which Kosta first had to clear of his most recent load of clean laundry. He was indifferent to his own untidiness; there had been books and magazines piled high on the dining table before they sat down to their meal, and even the chairs had a couple of weeks' worth of newspapers adorning their cushions. There were multiple spider plants and rubber plants crowded into every corner, their leaves coated with dust. And if Rachel wasn't mistaken, a small puddle of dog pee had greeted her at the entrance to the kitchen, where, on her arrival, Kosta's silky terrier, Cal, had first expressed his contempt for her.

Kosta clicked on his home-theatre-sized TV, and they watched *Law & Order SVU*. The episode featured a woman with multiple personality disorder (or D.I.D.—dissociative identity disorder—as the show's resident shrink politely corrected one of the detectives). "What a freak," said Kosta as the woman affected a harsh Russian accent and then, a moment later, insisted, in a high-pitched voice, that she was an eight-year-old child. Kosta kicked off his cowboy boots and rested his legs against the coffee table. His arm was around Rachel again. Cal looked at her disapprovingly, and climbed into Kosta's lap. For some reason the dog had been unhappy with Rachel from the moment she'd arrived, and so had been locked away all night in the bedroom. Now he was out on probation.

"Say something to me in Russian," Rachel requested.

"*Do svedanya*," said Kosta. "It's the only word I know."

Stroking the top of Cal's head, Rachel was rewarded with a growl. "Did you ever imagine the life you might have had if your parents hadn't…"

"Been summarily executed, who knows, their bodies tossed into a ditch somewhere?" said Kosta as Cal sunk his teeth into the fleshy tip of Rachel's thumb and she let out a small cry. "Very bad dog!" Kosta grumbled. "Did he break the skin?" he asked Rachel.

She sucked the tiny bubble of blood from her thumb. "It's nothing," she said. "As long as he doesn't have rabies, I mean." Sticking her tongue out at Cal, she thought about the long subway ride home. She knew Kosta had a car, a BMW that he kept out on the street because he didn't believe in paying for parking under any circumstance ever. Her mother had told Rachel, more than once, that wealthy people had their own crazy ideas about money—that, despite their vast resources, there were certain things they just wouldn't spring for. Even so, she wondered if Kosta would surrender his spot on the street and give her a lift home.

He kissed her slightly wounded thumb, took her hand, and led her into his bedroom without a word, using his foot to shut the door behind them. "I can't wait to see you," he said, his voice not much more than a whisper. On the other side of the door, Cal yipped insistently.

Later, as her fingers examined the wiry salt-and-pepper thicket of hair that covered Kosta's chest, Rachel told herself that he was in excellent shape for a middle-aged guy. (Not that she knew much about middle-aged anything.) His stomach wasn't paunchy in the least, and his arms and legs were long and muscular: when he'd wrapped them around her tightly, she'd gasped, and had to ask him to ease up.

"So you work out at the gym?" she said.

He pointed to a set of barbells on the floor at either side of the tall, army-green file cabinet where he kept his socks, underwear, and pajamas. "Forty minutes every morning," he said. "Hey, not bad for an old guy, right?"

"Not bad at all."

Flat on their backs, lying side by side, they held hands and ignored the scratching at the door. "I count this as one of the luckiest days of my unlucky life," Kosta announced.

Tears sprang to Rachel's eyes. *This wasn't a pity fuck,* she wanted to say, but, in truth, she didn't know *what* it was. She'd slept with a total of half a dozen men, mostly for the right reasons, she reflected. But was it even remotely possible that she'd slept with Kosta in part because his parents had been murdered by Stalin? Surely this couldn't be true. And yet surely there were worse reasons for allowing yourself to be seduced by a handsome man who had twenty years on you and hellish times in his past.

It was after two a.m. when she slipped back into her jeans and snapped her bra into place. Kosta stayed in bed, observing her closely. "Just watching you get dressed is a real turn-on," he said.

She smiled. "So…any chance you can give me a ride back uptown?"

No such luck.

"My parking spot is good until next Monday," Kosta explained. Downstairs on the street, he pressed a twenty dollar bill into her palm as she ducked into the first taxi that came her way. For an instant, closing her hand over the twenty, she felt the smallest bit like a hooker, albeit one with degrees from a couple of Ivy League universities. Kosta was tapping on the window now, and she lowered it. "It's just that finding a great parking spot is like a fucking miracle," he said apologetically. "Forgive me?"

"There's nothing to forgive," she heard herself say, and blew him a kiss, one of those gestures she rarely made use of.

When spring arrived, she'd accumulated more than a hundred pages of notes dictated by Kosta, but she felt less and less confident that these pages would add up to anything resembling a publishable book. Maybe a self-published book, but in all likelihood one that you might download for free on the Internet rather than buy at Barnes & Noble. Though Kosta's life fascinated her—especially his dismal childhood and adolescence, a couple of dissolute years at a community college, a stint in the army, his eventual success as a businessman, and two failed marriages to women he described as "nut jobs," one of whom was an African princess from Kenya—nothing could beat the single, seminal fact of his parents' execution. As she labored at Kosta's story one afternoon, Rachel thought of a quotation from Mark Twain that she loved. *There never was yet an uninteresting life. Inside of the dullest exterior there is a drama, a comedy and a tragedy.* If this was true—and she wholeheartedly believed that it was—then why was she having so much trouble shaping Kosta's extraordinary life into something worth reading about? Per their contract, which had been drawn up and notarized by Kosta's attorney, he had, to date, paid Rachel $10,000, a fact she tried not to think about whenever she spent the night in his bed. Certainly she found him a generous and considerate lover, one who knew how to deliver the lightest and most tender of kisses to her eyelids, whose fingers played skillfully along her body, bringing her moments of electrifying pleasure. Happily, there was that particular, necessary spark between them. But just as she was unsure of the book he was paying her to write, she wasn't yet convinced that she and Kosta would, in the long run, add up to anything at all. If prompted by Kosta, she would say that of course she loved him, though she didn't think she would ever say that she felt as if she'd been set on fire, as Kosta claimed to have been. She was attached to him, having been wooed by the story of his life, but she was also, she recently discovered, a little afraid of him.

At the tail end of the evening rush hour a few weeks earlier, as she and Kosta had boarded a packed subway car, he'd accidentally brushed shoulders with a well-dressed, briefcase-carrying woman who was trying to exit; when he murmured "excuse me," the woman cursed at him and gave him a deliberate shove. To Rachel's astonishment, he'd shoved her back. And roughly. He and the stranger exchanged fuck-yous, and then the woman took off. It was all over in less than a minute, and none of the other passengers seemed to have taken notice, but Rachel's heart was hammering away, and for an instant she couldn't catch her breath.

"What's *wrong* with you?" she hissed at Kosta.

"Are you fucking *kidding* me?" he said. "Didn't you see what she did to me?"

"Uh-huh, but I also saw what *you* did to *her*," Rachel said.

The two of them were gripping a pole to keep their balance as the subway car suddenly swayed sharply back and forth. She stared across the car. A guy wearing chipped, oxblood-colored nail polish extracted a slice of pizza from a cardboard box in his lap and bit into it zestfully, then took a swig from a bottle of Pepsi that had been wedged between his knees.

"She deserved it," Kosta insisted. "She left me no choice."

"That," said Rachel, "is patently untrue. Haven't you ever heard of turning the other cheek?"

Kosta smiled at her unpleasantly. "Hey, you know what? That's just what I did when Bobby or Dorothy used me as a punching bag. I turned the other cheek and prayed for someone to rescue me. And you know how well *that* turned out."

She couldn't win, Rachel saw. They'd been on their way downtown to Kosta's apartment, where she'd planned to make him linguine with scampi for dinner, but she no longer felt like doing anything for him. She couldn't forget the harshness with which he'd shoved the woman, though in all fairness to Kosta, the woman herself had been churlish and rude, and she'd been asking for trouble. Even so. On the other hand…Kosta had been savagely mistreated by his adoptive parents, and was, perhaps, permanently damaged in certain ways. She'd make the scampi, but after dinner, she'd go straight home, cheating them both of some exhilaratingly good sex.

One time, after they had finished making love and Kosta was channel-surfing the TV in his bedroom, they watched *CSI* in silence for a few minutes; on the screen, the coroner extracted a victim's heart and weighed it on a scale.

"How'd you like to do *that* for a living?" Rachel said. "Ick."

Kosta stretched an arm to the nightstand, and lit one of his infrequent cigarettes with a cheap, orange plastic lighter. Slouching against the headboard, he noisily exhaled a plume of smoke toward the ceiling. "You know, I've killed a couple of bad guys in my day," he confided, his eyes on the rising smoke.

"You're a real hoot, Kosta," said Rachel. She socked him lightly on the shoulder. "Hilarious."

"No, really, I mean it," Kosta said, still staring at the ceiling. "They were drug dealers working for the Russian mob."

"Come *on*. You think I'm an idiot?" Rachel said. The back of her neck suddenly felt prickly, and her palms were damp. "Like I'm supposed to believe you're a murderer?"

Kosta seemed affronted. "Not a murderer. I whacked a couple of very bad people, that's all." The TV was still on; there was a commercial for an Internet dating website being shown, and Kosta froze it with the remote. "Obviously," he said, "this isn't going into the book."

"Obviously," Rachel echoed, and laughed, though she wished she hadn't. She knew Kosta was pulling her leg, but she was tired of playing along.

"Want to know the first thing I thought of when I woke up the next morning?"

"Yeah, whatever."

"That I'd done the world a big favor." A length of dead ash fell from the cigarette onto his bare chest, but he didn't flinch.

Barefoot, seated upright on her bed with her laptop, struggling yet again with the opening chapters of Kosta's story, Rachel considered the $35,000 that would be deposited into her savings account if, and only if, she could finish the damn book. *The damn book*—there was no other way to think of it. Always a stellar student and a hard-working, conscientious employee, she'd never really failed at anything, but this ill-conceived project had fiasco written all over it. It made her sick with humiliation to think of giving up, and even sicker to ponder the $35,000 and how it might have enhanced her life. She'd been fantasizing, recently, of joining Lara, her best friend from Brown, on a leisurely tour of Italy—Rome, Florence, Venice, Milan, Naples. She was thirty, only weeks away from thirty-one, old enough to have accomplished something substantial in her life. Instead, she'd held a succession of disappointing jobs and spent the better part of a year on a project that appealed to the vanity of a middle-aged businessman who had mistakenly convinced her she could turn his rather remarkable story into something of artistic merit. Though this was the man she claimed to love, she'd yet to introduce him to her parents or even to a single one of her friends. She told herself this was because they wouldn't be able to appreciate his generosity and devotion to her (a thick bracelet of pink, white, and yellow gold he bought for her at Tiffany; the surprising, elegant meals he treated her to at Nobu; the sweetness with which he said goodnight to her every evening over the phone when they were apart), but would instead regard him merely as the pony-tailed weirdo who showered in the ladies' room an elevator ride away from his apartment. (In a moment of weakness and poor judgment, she'd shared the details of both the men's room and ladies' room with her mother and Lara, each of whom reacted with disbelief, followed by uneasy laughter.)

Her cell phone rang; it was her mother, and Rachel briefly debated whether to answer it. Loving though she was, her mother had a gift for exasperating her with her pointed questions and her unquenchable thirst for every last detail about her life. Warily, Rachel picked up and said hello.

Her mother was calling from her midtown office to ask if Rachel would bring Kosta to the brunch she was making in honor of Rachel's birthday in a couple of weeks. It seemed to Rachel that every birthday in their family had been celebrated with the same tableful of assorted freshly warmed bagels, platters of lox and cream cheese, and her father's soupy, undercooked broccoli quiche. And a Double Chocolate Indulgence cake from Baskin-Robbins that had to be thawed a little in the microwave just to get a knife through it. This, Rachel saw, was what her parents would always be most comfortable with—they were, at heart, authentic suburbanites who had been raised outside of Philadelphia, and who, despite their successful dental practice here in the city and their apartment on Riverside Drive, could not fathom the beauty of that miso-glazed black cod at Nobu.

"It's your birthday, sweetheart," her mother said reasonably. "Just bring the guy and let us have a look at him finally."

"Well, I don't know," Rachel said, abruptly closing her laptop, as if her mother had snuck up beside her, and, over her shoulder, begun reading all about the crap poor Kosta had, in 1959, been subjected to at the hands of the beastly Dorothy and Bobby.

"What's the worst that could happen? If I don't like him, I'll keep it to myself," her mother promised. "Look, we've met all your other boyfriends over the years. What's the big deal about meeting this one?"

"He's not my boyfriend," Rachel snapped. "You don't call a fifty-five-year-old man a boyfriend, okay?"

"Wait, he's *fifty-five?*" her mother said, considering this piece of news with astonishment. "When you told us he was middle-aged, I thought you meant forty, forty-one...Rachel, what are you *doing?*"

"His parents were executed by Stalin!" Rachel shrieked. "Stop criticizing him!" A moment later, she was sobbing.

Suddenly exhausted, too tired even to rise from her bed to look for a tissue, she wiped her eyes with the pair of argyle socks she'd worn yesterday and tossed onto the floor before going to sleep.

"*Joseph* Stalin?" her mother said, and Rachel could tell that she was impressed.

"Well, not Stalin personally, but on his personal orders anyway."

Her mother cleared her throat. "I'm speechless," she said.

"And… his ex-wife was an African princess," Rachel said recklessly.

"Stalin was married to an African princess?"

"*Kosta*," Rachel said, instantly regretting the impatience in her voice. "He's had a pretty incredible life, don't you think?"

———

After a sleepover at Kosta's, on the morning of her birthday brunch, Rachel had her first shower in the ladies' room. With Kosta leading the way, she hurried from his apartment, down the corridor and into the elevator, dressed in his plaid bathrobe that swished around her ankles and his enormous fuzzy brown slippers that were meant to resemble the paws of a bear and that swam on her size-six feet. When they arrived at the fourth floor, Kosta darted into the ladies' room for a quick look around, then signaled to her that the coast was clear.

"No worries. There's never a soul in here on the weekends, of that I can assure you," he said. He helped Rachel out of his robe and kissed each of her breasts before turning on the water for her. He'd brought his shower caddy along; a selection of two different shampoos and conditioners were available for her choosing, and a bar of Dove For Sensitive Skin that was still encased in its cardboard packaging. "Just for you," said Kosta. "I knew this day would come." He stood guard while she shampooed and conditioned her hair behind the frosted glass, and then, like a limo driver at the service of his passenger, reached politely for her hand as she stepped from the shower. A plush, sweet-smelling towel awaited her, and before she dried off completely, she couldn't help but catch a glimpse of herself in the mirrored wall, partially misted with steam, that rose above the sinks. Kosta was looking at her, too, and then an idea came to both of them. Pressed against the wall, a damp towel lining her back, she felt the warmth of Kosta's breath on her neck. There was no lock on the ladies' room door; if someone had walked in on them, Rachel would have wanted to shoot herself. But it was a quiet Sunday morning in August, and they were all alone in the city.

Kosta's black sapphire BMW M6 was parked directly in front of his building, and he sighed in contentment as they settled into the car. With a touch of a button, the convertible top eased itself down smoothly behind them. They were out of the Village quickly and flying up the West Side Highway, and the smile on Kosta's face seemed joyful. Clearly he loved his new car and the sultry August wind blowing in their faces. Rachel held onto her hair with both hands and wished he would put the top up and turn on the air-conditioning, though she wouldn't have dreamed of saying so and spoiling his pleasure. On her lap was the large, extravagant bouquet of flowers he'd bought for her parents; on her wrist was the starkly elegant black-faced Movado he'd given her for her birthday. She could guess how expensive it was and the thought rattled her, though not so much that she contemplated returning it to him. His generosity was lavish; how could you fault a man for that?

"Thirty-one years old," he said. "A mere slip of a girl. Rejoice in thy youth, missy!" They were on Riverside Drive now, only a few blocks from her parents' apartment, and on the lookout for a parking space.

"Cut it out," Rachel told him. She didn't like it when he drew attention to the difference in their ages; the truth was, it saddened her.

"Let's see, when I was thirty-one, I was married to my ex, Joanne, and miserable. And I mean *miserable*. All she could ever think about was this ridiculous—"

"Isn't that a spot over there?" Rachel interrupted.

A woman her age was standing in front of an awning watching over her toddler in a stroller. " 'You're a grand old flaaag,'" she prompted loudly, and her little boy sang, " 'You're a high fly-ing flag!'"

"Fire hydrant," Kosta pointed out. "No good."

As the BMW pulled away, Rachel could hear the child in the stroller shrieking, " 'And for-ev-er in peace may you waaave...'"

"Cute kid," said Kosta cheerfully.

They'd circled her parents' building four times but there wasn't a single parking spot to be had. Hydrants sprouted cruelly from every open space, it seemed, and Kosta's mood had darkened. "We have a serious situation at hand," he said. "My hopes have dimmed."

Was he talking about a parking space or a malignant tumor?

"We'll just have to put it in a garage," Rachel said. "And of course I'll pay for it." She held her breath, and waited.

"You'll do no such thing," said Kosta. "I'll let you out, and I'll meet you upstairs as soon as I find a spot."

"I'm not leaving you," she said, as if he were going off to do battle with a dangerous adversary.

"Git," said Kosta. He handed her the flowers for her parents. "See you later, birthday girl."

She went upstairs and into the warmth of her family, which included her 84-year-old grandmother, two aunts and uncles, and her brother, all of whom seemed disappointed to see that she'd arrived without Kosta. Rachel explained that he was looking for parking, and her relatives clucked sympathetically. Everyone was in agreement with her mother when she acknowledged that it was always a problem finding parking on the Upper

West Side, even in summer, when much of the neighborhood was supposedly out in the Hamptons for the weekend.

"Why can't this young man of yours just park in a garage?" her grandmother asked. "What's wrong with *that*?"

He's not a young man, Rachel wanted to say. *He's set in his ways.*

"He may very well end up in that garage," her father said grimly. "Like it or not, sometimes you just don't have a choice."

It was decided that they would wait for Kosta, even though the assortment of bagels had been warmed in the oven and would, undoubtedly and in no time, turn cold and stony.

Her mother put out large bowls of fat-free potato chips and salt-free pretzels, in deference to those who had to worry about high cholesterol or hypertension. As for Rachel and her brother, they who liked their chips relatively oily and their pretzels full of salt, well, tough break.

Forty-five minutes passed and the voice mail and text messages Rachel had left on Kosta's BlackBerry went unanswered.

"Good luck to you with that crazy boyfriend!" her grandmother called after her when Rachel left the apartment to find him.

He was double-parked in front of the building, his face lowered into the steering wheel.

She came around to the driver's side. "Hey," she said, tugging at his ponytail. "I left you three messages."

He lifted his head and gazed at her sorrowfully. "Looks like I'm going to have to give up."

"Thank God!" she said, relieved that he had, at last, come to his senses. "There's a garage a few blocks away, off West End. My father says it'll only cost about twenty-five dollars for a couple of hours, so if you don't want to spring for it, please just let me take care of it, all right?" she pleaded.

"I can't let you do that," Kosta said. "Absolutely not. Listen, I'm going home. Please give my apologies to your parents." Gently, he placed his hand over her arm, the one sporting that lovely new Movado that sat a little too tightly around her wrist. "You understand, don't you?"

Shutting her eyes against his blindness, his mulish refusal to pay the measly twenty-five bucks, she allowed herself to fully evoke, as she never had before, the night of his parents' execution—that young mother and father, younger even than Rachel herself, roused from their warm feather bed, the chilly steel of pistols shoved in their faces, Kosta's mother crying out in terror for her baby dreaming in his crib in the room next door, his father shouting *Who are you?* but immediately recognizing those ruthless strangers pounding on their door after midnight wanting only to destroy their innocent, ordinary lives. How readily Rachel imagined all of it, and the long, long way from there to here, to Riverside Drive and this intractable man who, no matter what, refused to pay for a damn parking space. This man who wanted to know if she understood.

ACKNOWLEDGMENTS

My heartfelt thanks to Michelle Toth, Andrew Goldstein, Eliyanna Kaiser, and, as always, George Axelrod.

photo by George Axelrod

MARIAN THURM is the author of three other short story collections and six novels; her novel *The Clairvoyant* was a *New York Times* Notable Book. Her short stories have appeared in the *New Yorker*, the *Atlantic*, the *Michigan Quarterly*, the *Southampton Review*, and many other magazines, and have been included in *The Best American Short Stories*, and numerous other anthologies. Her books have been translated into Japanese, Swedish, Dutch, and German. She has taught creative writing at Yale, Barnard College, the Writing Institute at Sarah Lawrence College, and in the MFA programs at Columbia University and Brooklyn College.

CPSIA information can be obtained at www.ICGtesting.com
Printed in the USA
LVOW11s1505261015

459778LV00006B/752/P